Escape from Frog Pond

By

Caelin Paul

Copyright © 2023 by Caelin Paul.

All rights reserved. No part of this book may be used or reproduced in any form whatsoever without written permission except in the case of brief quotations in critical articles or reviews.

Printed in the United States of America.

For more information, or to book an event, contact :
Dr. Caelin Paul
E-Mail : caelinpaul@gmail.com
http://www.amazon.com/author/caelinpaul

Book design by DOCIDE LLC
Cover design by DOCIDE LLC

ISBN – Hardback : 979-8-9873480-7-9
ISBN - Paperback: 979-8-9873480-0-0
ISBN – E-Book : 979-8-9873480-1-7
ISBN – Audio : 979-8-9873480-2-4

First Edition: May, 2023

Acknowledgment

For my best friend Anna who has been by my side through many difficult days.

Chapters

Frog Pond	....	*1*
The Stream	....	*9*
The Citadel	....	*18*
The Windmill	....	*32*
The Cabins	....	*44*
The Schoolhouse	....	*53*
The Mountain	....	*66*
The Hospital	....	*80*
The Eyrie	....	*90*
The Workshop	....	*107*
The Statue	....	*119*
Homecoming	....	*123*
Frog Pond	....	*131*
Epilogue	....	*142*

Cast of Characters

Artur -- Prince of the Eagles

Can'tsi -- Matriarch of Frog Pond family

Doci -- Brave Adventurer from Frog Pond

Emma -- Friendly Mountain Pony

Fledge -- Friendly Eagle from Eagle Nest

I'llsi -- Patriarch of Frog Pond family

Isaac -- Ferret – Gate-Keeper at the Eyrie

King Egron -- King of the Eagles

Litho -- Wise Bull-frog

Logabin -- Business owner of Logabin's Cabins

LogBook -- Second Name for We'llsi

LogDoc -- Medical Doctor for the Woodland

Logger -- Master Carpenter

Cast of Characters

LogFarm -- Potato Farmer on the Confluence

Logic -- School-Teacher on the Confluence

Logit -- Endurance Racing Champion

LogJam -- Court Chef of the Eagle Nest

Logo -- Second Name for You'llsi

Logout -- Extreme Sports Enthusiast

Mr. Beaver -- Patriarch of the Beaver family

Oscar -- Logabin's Business Partner

We'llsi -- Doci's Brother on Frog Pond

You'llsi -- Doci's Sister on Frog Pond

Frog Pond

Once … No … "Many upon a time…" there lived five little frogs. From sunrise to sunset, they sat upon a log near the river bank. Every day the hot summer sun beat down mercilessly upon their little froggy backs. Sweat poured down tiny arms, perspiration streamed along powerful legs. At precisely 2:00p.m., with the sun at its fiercest, all five frogs *decided* to jump into the cool water. The question is, at 2:01p.m., how many frogs remained sat upon the log?

The answer...**FIVE!** You see deciding to jump into the water is not the same as taking action. Our little amphibious friends had not yet developed the capacity to **"DOCIDE."** So, from dawn to dusk, the family of five huddled together on their gnarly log gazing forlornly into the calm crystal waters of the pond.

Doci, the youngest froggy in the family, often became bored of the daily routine. He amused himself lashing his tentacle tongue at the ubiquitous gnats and mosquitos that chose to share his wetland abode. No one on the log ever moved, spoke, or did anything of interest. Doci, determined to be the very best frog possible, followed the example of his brother and sister. With concentration and extreme focus, he sought to mimic the statuesque qualities of the older frogs.

Occasionally, the frog pond welcomed visitors. Doci loved these rare events that helped break the monotony of sitting, croaking, sitting, croaking, and more sitting. One morning in the late Spring, the beaver family returned from vacation. Mr. Beaver was a friendly soul and always courteous to the Frog family. Of course, the frozen amphibians rarely acknowledged his hearty greetings. Doci loved the Beaver family. The beavers were excellent swimmers and seemed to glide effortlessly through the water. They were industrious and always working on the lodge in the northwest corner of the pond. Laughter and babbling conversation displaced the morose silence. Doci watched every movement and yearned to play in the water beside the exuberant rodents.

One day, Doci got up the courage to whisper a question to his brother We'llsi.

"Hey, We'llsi, why do we sit on a log all day and not go anywhere?"

We'llsi issued an impatient belch. "Doci, this is what we do. We sit on our log and guard the pond."

Doci pondered this response for several minutes. "Why do we guard the pond?" he asked.

We'llsi shrugged, "I don't know, why don't you ask your sister You'llsi."

Doci turned to his left and nudged his sister. "You'llsi why do we sit all day on the log guarding the pond?"

You'llsi smiled down at him. "Oh Doci, you cute polliwog. We sit here all day because that is what frogs do."

Doci found himself growing increasingly impatient. "But why? The beavers do not sit like rocks all day long."

You'llsi sighed, "perhaps you should ask momma."

Doci stretched his front leg around his sister and tapped Momma Can'tsi on the shoulder. "Momma why do we do nothing all day long?"

Can'tsi wore oversize sunglasses to protect her eyes from the fierce sunshine. Years of gazing at the water had blinded her. "Oh Doci, all creatures of the world have their role to play. Our role is to sit on this log and make sure we don't fall in the water."

Doci started to get frustrated. "But why?" he croaked.

Can'tsi smiled as only momma frogs with sunglasses can. "Go ask your father. He has sat on the log the longest."

Doci loved and respected his father. I'llsi squatted intimidatingly at the far end of the log beside his older brother We'llsi. Sidling up beside his brother he leaned across and looked up into the bulbous eyes of his father.

"Papa, why do we sit on the log all day every day? Why do we not play in the water like the beaver family?"

Papa I'llsi stretched his giant legs and for a moment his immense frame blotted out the sun. "Doci, it is a dangerous world out there. We are safe on this log. Once upon a time there were eight other frogs that also lived in the pond. One day a massive rainstorm washed away their logs. They disappeared over the beaver dam and on down the river never to be heard from again. So, we sit here and guard the pond. If another storm comes, we will be ready." Papa I'llsi settled down into a crouch and once more transformed into an immoveable rock. "Now back to work young Doci," bellowed the rock.

Doci resumed his silent vigil over the playful activities of the beaver family. Doci loved his family. We'llsi and You'llsi were kind siblings. Momma Can'tsi and Papa I'llsi were solid parents who balanced the log perfectly. But Doci knew in his heart of hearts there had to be more to life. Hours of guard duty gave the little frog plenty of time to engage his creative imagination. He often wondered what life beyond the beaver dam would be like. Since the conversation with Papa, Doci could just not stop thinking about the fate of eight frogs swept away in the historic flood Papa mentioned.

Later in the summer, Mr. Beaver popped by to pay his respects to Papa and his froggy family. "Hello Mr. I'llsi. Greetings to you and your lovely family. We are getting ready to move down stream to get the winter lodge ready. Summer has been especially warm so the snows might be deep."

Doci's ears perked up. Snow, what was that? He watched with sadness as the Beaver family packed up their little suitcases and shut up the lodge. With a cheery wave, Mr. Beaver disappeared over the dam and peace and deafening quietness consumed the pond once more.

Two days passed uneventfully. On the third day following the departure of the Beavers, large raindrops attacked the pond. The rains were coming. Throughout the thunderstorms, the lightning, the monsoons, and the rising waters, the froggy family remained transfixed upon their log. After one particularly glorious rain storm, Doci looked up to see the most beautiful sight he had ever before beheld. A luminescent arc of color caressed the horizon above the beaver dam. The colors of the rainbow burst vibrantly in a powerful contrast to the sweeping black clouds that lingered in the east. Doci felt a strange emotion. Within his tiny chest heartbeats rippled with a startling exuberance. Before he knew what was happening, long legs stretched upwards and suddenly feet no longer touched the submersible tree trunk. Time stood motionless as Doci's body propelled itself into the air. Eyes of the family looked on in horror as Doci landed with an almighty SPLASH in the crystal waters of the pond. A powerful exhilaration and electricity prickled over his sinews as he swam toward the dam. Hopping onto the beaver lodge, Doci took one last look back over his shoulder. He waved passionately a fond farewell to his family. Turning back towards the rainbow, Doci took in a huge breath. With the DO-CISION made, Doci had a new direction in life –

FORWARDS. With that, the little froglet
launched himself into the great wide unknown.

The Stream

Doci let the water wash over him. The rain continued to fall. The little frog barely noticed. Never in his life had he felt so free, so alive, so energized. The stream cut a path through a narrow valley and the fast-flowing current posed a stark contrast to the placid waters of the pond. Doci soon discovered he was not alone in the deluge. There hurtling along beside him were branches, logs, leaves, and all manner of fishy creatures. At one point, a large leather boot drifted nonchalantly by. Doci looked down at his spindly webbed feet and he could not help but feel a little uneasy. Whoever owned this boot must have been a giant.

Dark clouds thundered through the sky. Rain continued to splay up and down the narrow waterway. After several hours the contours of the stream began to change. The channel grew wider and large boulders randomly made unsuccessful attempts to stymie the exuberant current. Doci started to find himself buffeted against the glass-smooth walls of these obstacles. Fortunately, the polished surfaces caused little problems for a fit, young frog.

Suddenly, Doci came upon a particularly awkward patch of nature. Massive granite batholiths erupted from the frothy waters. These natural monuments lay staggered periodically down the stream. Little did Doci know but the stream had now in fact become a river. The currents here did not cooperate as they had closer to the frog pond. Doci bounced up against another rock. This time something strange occurred. Doci suddenly realized the water had stopped moving him forward. He kicked his spindly legs as hard as he possibly could. Nothing. He froggy paddled his arms feverishly. Nothing. All around him the current surged downriver but Doci seemed stuck. The little frog grew increasingly perplexed at his predicament.

Doci studied his situation. A pragmatic and studious little fellow, he searched for a solution. The water swirled around the boulder creating a vortex. Despite the fast-moving stream, the downstream water seemed to be fighting against a current that encircled the rock. The harder, Doci fought against the current the more tired his little frame became. If he stopped struggling against the flow, he found himself sinking. After a couple of hours, Doci started to feel the first inkling of fear. Surely, it would not be prudent to give up. Who heard of a frog drowning? Sure, there were rumors of cannibals from France drowning frogs in boiling water. But, here in the wide-open arms of Mother Nature? No, Doci refused to accept the fate of drowning.

Problem-solving went into overdrive and Doci noticed that an occasional wayward branch sometimes got driven into the vortex. More often than not this debris would get sucked under the surface and smashed into smithereens along the rocky bottom. Doci concocted a plan. If he could just lever himself onto the edge of a branch, he might be able to use his extraordinary leaping prowess to jump from the branch to the rock and back into the current. He didn't have to wait long for a leafy bough to swim on by. This piece of forest debris was just the right size. Doci heaved himself onto the sinking log. Just as the swirling vortex threatened to suck them both into the watery abyss, Doci coiled himself into a ball. Exercising a mighty eccentric muscle contraction, Doci catapulted himself high into the air. He bounced off the polished granite, arched his body and performed a perfect dive into the raging waters. He swallowed a lungful of sandy sediment. When he resurfaced, he found himself moving and free of the eddy.

Every limb, muscle, tendon, and bone ached. Suddenly he felt very sleepy. His leaping trajectory had sent his course toward the riverbank. The water flowed more evenly and quietly here. Weeping willows stretched delicately to the surface. Sandy banks ran down to the river edge welcoming the little frog. Doci felt his belly scrape against the shore. Dragging his exhausted body up onto the bank, he promptly fell asleep among the tall bulrushes.

Doci woke late the next morning. Every muscle ached and bruises littered his green-skinned frame. For the first time he began to question leaving the safe refuge of the frog pond. The rain had stopped falling and sun peeked between the leaving storm clouds. Doci noticed several accommodating logs close to the river bank. Choosing a sturdy platform, he took up his post and closed his eyes for a long mid-morning nap. Mid-morning quickly became afternoon, then evening. Nightfall extended his torpor and before he knew it the days became an endless exercise in stagnant routine. Soon the motivation for adventure faded and Doci settled into a life of purposelessness.

This could very well have been the end of our story had it not been for a chance encounter with Lithobates Catesbeiana.

Litho was an enormous Bullfrog who had been watching Doci from the moment he had first entered the eddy. Admittedly, it was a curious thing to see a Northern Green Frog this far from the freshwater pond and all alone in the wilderness. Everyday Litho watched as Doci took up his post on the log then returned to the safety of the bulrushes at night. At least the young frog knew the importance of hiding from the night-time predators. This patch of the river hosted the hunting grounds for the notorious snowy owls.

Although, Doci always chose the same log to sit on during the day, he moved his night-time bed frequently. So it was that Doci unwittingly encroached upon the bedroom of Lithobates Catesbeiana.

Doci bedded down for the night and was just about to fall asleep when a deep booming voice frightened him from his slumber.

"Hello little frog," bellowed Litho.

A startled Doci swung around and found himself face-to-face with the largest American Bullfrog he had ever encountered. "Hello Sir. I am sorry for disturbing you. I did not realize that any other frogs lived here."

"No worries my tiny green friend. It is a pleasure to have company." Litho settled back down into his bulrush nest. "I could not help but be intrigued with your courageous battle with the eddy," said Litho. "You are a very strong little frog. What are you doing so far from home?"

Doci experienced the unfamiliar pangs of homesickness. "Sir, I watched the Beavers leave and wanted to see where they go every year."

Litho chuckled, "you are indeed a strange fellow. Who heard of a frog chasing a beaver family downstream? What do you hope to find on your big adventure?"

Doci considered the question for a moment. "Papa told me that eight frogs were once washed away from Frog Pond. I wanted to find out what happened to them."

"Well now, that is an exciting reason to leave the pond." Litho itched his chin for a moment. "You know I did hear about a frog who years ago conquered the 'Citadel.'"

"The Citadel? What is that?" asked Doci.

"The Citadel," Litho continued, "is an impossible challenge that has taken the lives of countless hundreds of frogs. The greatest frog athletes from all over the land meet to contest the race every year. The Citadel is a very tall tower with over 300 steps. Often 100 athletes start the race but no one ever finishes. But there was one that achieved the impossible. I believe she also came from Frog Pond."

Doci felt an upsurge of excitement. "I would very much like to meet this frog. Perhaps I could even race at the Citadel."

Litho smiled, "well my young friend, after watching you battle the eddy, I am sure you would be brave enough to enter the race. However, in order to achieve greatness, one must be prepared to enter the current and be brave enough to stay in the moving water. I have been watching you these last few weeks. The eddy seems to have stolen your purpose. Now the safety and security of the river bank has stolen your drive. If you want to take on the Citadel, you must be prepared to take risks. You must be prepared to be courageous. You must be prepared to have endurance and not give up when you get stuck. So, my little friend, are you prepared to enter the current and commit to the moving water?"

Doci experienced the selfsame excitement that motivated him to leave the sanctuary of Frog Pond. How could he have given up so quickly? In that moment, he made a quiet commitment to always follow the moving water no matter how fierce the current, how difficult to navigate the eddies, and how tempting the security of the river bank.

Doci extended a webbed paw to the Bullfrog. "Sir, it has been an honor to make your acquaintance. I will continue to search out those who left the Frog Pond and I will enter this race at the Citadel."

"That's the spirit my young friend," said Litho. "Sunrise will be upon us in just a few hours. I suggest that you shut your eyes and get some rest. You will most definitely require all your wits about you on your journey. Even little green frogs need 9-10 hours of sleep a night to be effective adventurers." Litho patted Doci's head. "I will wake you in the morning and send you on your way. Goodnight little one."

Doci promptly fell asleep dreaming of white-water rivers and elegant white spires reaching high into the clouds.

The Citadel

True to his word, Litho woke Doci in the early morning. The old Bullfrog had created a small picnic lunch of fruit fly sandwiches and pickled mosquitoes. Litho packed up the bag and hoisted it on to Doci's shoulders.

"Have to make sure you keep your strength up," Litho said. "Now remember what I told you. Always stay in the moving water. Your life will always have a purpose if you commit to action and remain in the flow. If life gets tough, choose a different direction or a different speed, but remain in the flow."

"Yes Sir, I most certainly will," stated Doci.

With a hearty breakfast in his tummy, and lunch upon his back, Doci entered the river. As the pace of the water picked up, Doci just had a chance to raise a farewell hand and holler a farewell thank you. In seconds, Litho and the riverbank were gone.

Doci kept an eye out for all the landmarks Litho had given him in the instructions. Sure enough, on the west bank a grove of crab apple trees. On the east bank a capsized row boat with a gaping hole in the hull. A half mile further downstream, Doci came upon the Confluence. Two rivers flowed into one and a large island dissected the junction. Even from a distance, Doci could make out the majestic white spiraling tower of the Citadel. Litho had described the building as a deserted church in the middle of an island. This had to be the place.

Doci navigated the shallows and hopped on to the shore. An overgrown path meandered its way upwards between an avenue of enormous aspens. Taking in a deep breath, Doci hitched up his little backpack and hopped down the trail. In no time at all the church came into view. Paint peeled back from aging walls and pigeons flew in and out of broken window panes. Wooden steps creaked ominously as Doci approached the tall paneled entranceway. A small hole, frog sized, had been carved into the heavy-set doors. Doci entered and was immediately confronted by a bespectacled toad with a purple Mohawk.

"Welcome to the Citadel little green frog," stated the toad. "The competition doesn't start until 8a.m. tomorrow. Spectators have been arriving for weeks in order to take their positions on the high steps. I am afraid you will have to camp out on the low steps for the race. Admission will be two fruit flies."

"Excuse me ma'am I am not here to watch, I am here to sign up. How much is the race entry?"

The purple Mohawk peered down at Doci over the horn-rimmed spectacles. "You are a racer? Jumping dragonflies. You must be the smallest frog we have ever seen start the Citadel. Oh, and racers get in free." The toad smiled revealing black gums and a slew of rotting teeth. "We don't see too many Northern Green Frogs down here on the Confluence. Although, the legendary Ichy was a Green Frog."

"Ichy? Who is Ichy?" asked Doci.

Mohawk looked aghast. "Who is Ichy? What log have you been hiding under? Ichy is a legend. Ichy is the only frog in a hundred years to complete the Citadel run."

"Aah, Litho told me about a frog that managed to get to the top."

"Get to the top indeed…all 300 steps without ever pausing for a sip of water or a mosquito cracker. Absolutely incredible it was. She set a new world record of 302 stomps."

"302 stomps? What is that?" asked Doci.

Mohawk looked aghast yet again. "You really are from the boonies. Stomps are how we measure time here. Once the race starts everyone along the race course stomps their feet in time to a drum. Most frogs do not last 100 stomps, only the most athletic get to 200 stomps, and Ichy is the only froggy to manage 300 stomps. Can you imagine she climbed 300 steps in 302 stomps. Marvelous it was, legendary, never to be repeated, at least not in my lifetime."

"I bet I can beat 300 stomps," Doci said out loud.

Mohawk burst into fits of hearty guffaws. "You last 300 stomps? Oh, how funny. You really are a brave little frog." Mohawk moved away to talk to a large yellow lake frog who had just walked through the door.

With nothing better to do, Doci returned to the churchyard. The sun still played on the horizon and Doci found a shady tree under which to sit and eat lunch. The fruit fly snacks were extremely pleasant. He saved two for the morning not wanting to race the Citadel on an empty stomach. After filling his belly, Doci left the churchyard and wandered into the woods.

After several minutes of hopping, Doci came upon a tiny door set into the trunk of a silver birch tree. Above the door, a small plaque read "ICHY!" Consumed with curiosity, Doci knocked on the door. No response. As he turned to go, his nose bumped into another nose. An old woman with streaks of grey perforating wrinkled green stood in front of him. The strange frog extended a webbed appendage.

"Hi, I'm Ichy!"

Doci smiled broadly. "Hi Ichy, I am Doci."

Ichy smiled back then took a key out of her bag and unlocked the door. She beckoned Doci inside and shut the door.

The house was very simply furnished with two chairs, a table, and a carved log for a bed. On the mantelpiece sat a large trophy with the words *"Citadel Champion-302 Stomps"* engraved upon its base. Doci reached up and ran his fingers along the base of the silver cup. "You are the Champion Ichy everyone talks about. Tell me about it?"

Ichy stood by the water bowl preparing a delicious snack of mosquito larvae.

Doci, spoke up again. "I saw the toad with the Mohawk today and I entered the race. Could you give me some advice?"

Still no response from Ichy. Doci just stared at the little old lady as she pottered around the kitchen. Could this really be the highly tuned athlete that conquered the Citadel?

Ichy noticed the confused expression on Doci's face. Stepping across the room she took Doci's face in her two hands and said, "Sorry I cannot hear you because I am deaf. I only understand what you are saying if I can see and read your lips."

Doci nodded understanding. "Thank you for letting me come visit. I am going to race the Citadel tomorrow. I would love some tips."

Ichy smiled knowingly and a fiery energy darted across her eyes. "You are a Northern Green Frog. If anyone has a chance to get to the top it will be you. You see we are light on our feet and use much less energy than the other toads and frogs."

"Is that how you won the race? Were you light on your feet?" asked Doci.

Ichy laughed merrily. "Oh no, I am actually a very clumsy little frog."
"How did you get to the top?" asked Doci.

"Aah, that is a secret, but I will share it with you tomorrow at the start line. For now, you must eat and get some sleep."

Doci slept very well on a full stomach and dreamed of holding aloft a silver cup. When

Ichy woke him early in the morning he was still dreaming of victory.

"Are you ready to run little green frog?" Ichy asked.

"You bet," answered back Doci.

"Then let's get to the church on time," laughed Ichy,

A party atmosphere filled the church. Doci had never before seen so many frogs gathered in one place. Literally thousands of amphibians lined the spiraling stairwell. Mohawk pottered around putting all of the contestants on the start line. All-in-all there were forty-three frogs contesting the annual Citadel challenge. A significant hush permeated the crowd as Ichy pushed through the throng to the start line. The reverence of the crowd was palpable. Ichy sidled up beside Doci and thrust two tiny marshmallows into his hand. Doci stared at the white fluffy treats. He did not feel hungry after his hearty breakfast but he did not want to be rude and decline the gift. He lifted a marshmallow to his mouth and Ichy promptly slapped his hand. Taking the marshmallows, she stuffed them into Doci's ears.

Doci immediately went deaf. He could see the crowd and his competitors but he could not hear a thing. Ichy gave him a big thumbs up and disappeared into the crowd.

Moments later, Mohawk stepped up to give the racers final instructions. Doci could not understand a word. He shrugged his shoulders and concentrated on his other senses. A large otter sat off to the side with a gigantic drum between his legs. Mighty drumsticks began to rise and fall. Simultaneously thousands of frogs started to stomp their feet in unison with the drumbeats. Doci could not hear the drum but he could most definitely feel the collective stomp.

Doci had become so transfixed with the drumming and the stomping that he failed to notice the race had begun. Suddenly, Ichy stood beside him and gave him a less than gentle push towards the staircase.

The first few steps were wide and not very tall. In less than a minute Doci caught the tail end of the race. On the lower steps there were literally thousands of frogs cheering on the athletes. As the race continued higher, the ranks of spectators thinned out and the hand waving seemed to be differently animated. Doci concentrated on the vibrations of the stomp and started to bound two steps for every stomp.

On the 100th step a frog choir seemed to be singing. Several competitors had clearly given up and more than a handful looked close to death. By the half-way point, Doci calculated he must be in the top 10. His little feet were getting sore but the furious hand-waving spectators kept him going. At the 200th step someone had placed a scoreboard. A noble looking salamander placed a number 4 by Doci's name. Spurred on by this revelation that only three racers were ahead, Doci continued to stay on the stomp beat.

Fifty steps later the crowd was growing ever more boisterous. They didn't seem to be smiling as much and large pools of frogs were surrounding two participants that no longer looked very alive. The final rival succumbed to step number 287. Doci could now see the finish line. A small open-air platform beside a massive brass bell beckoned. Doci's little heart beat faster than a hummingbird's wings. Sweat poured from his bulbous forehead and muscles he never even knew he had threatened to go on strike. With a surge of adrenaline, Doci powered to the finish line. No sooner had he flopped across the final step than the church bells, courtesy of two chameleon bell ringers, pealed out across the Confluence.

Doci passed out exhausted and vaguely knew the sensation of being lifted onto an uncomfortable litter. When he eventually awoke, he discovered the familiar surroundings of Ichy's treehouse. What an amazing dream. He had won the Citadel race. Now he knew he was ready to compete.

Doci stepped out of bed and promptly collapsed onto the floor. His little legs could barely support his weight. "I guess it was not a dream after all." Out of the corner of his eye he caught a glimpse of a silver cup poking out of his backpack. Pulling it out onto his lap he read the inscription… ***"Citadel Champion-298 Stomps."***

"I am so proud of you." Ichy appeared behind him and patted Doci on the head.

"Everyone said it could never be done, but look you went under 300 stomps after waiting at least 10 stomps before even starting the race."

Doci turned to face his friend. "Thank you for all of your help. But, I have to ask...the marshmallows?"

Ichy smiled knowingly. "Aah yes, the secret weapon. My real name is Logit, but after my Citadel race everyone started calling me Ichy. You see, I.C.H.Y. is initials for 'I Can't Hear You.' Did you notice anything different about the spectators at the top of the stairs?"

Doci thought for a moment. "Actually, I did. They didn't seem as happy and excited about the race. But they still seemed to be cheering loudly and waved their hands a lot."

"That's where the marshmallows come in handy," said Ichy, Those, spectators are the naysayers. They are not actually encouraging you at all. They are shouting at you to stop, to turn back, to not continue. They are the ones that believe the Citadel is impossible and can only lead to injury or death. You won the race, like me thinking you were being cheered on instead of being told the task was impossible."

Doci suddenly burst into fits of giggles. "Ichy you are amazing. Thank you for the marshmallows."

"Doci it is my pleasure and I can't think of a nicer frog to beat my record."

"Ichy, can I ask you one more question?"

"Sure Doci," she replied.

"Why did you never return to Frog Pond? One day there were eight frogs on a log and then the next day my Papa says they were gone."

"My family all got swept downriver and we decided to follow the flow wherever it would take us. My brother LogFarm lives downstream near the windmill. He always wanted to be a farmer and persuaded an old badger to let him farm potatoes."

"Do you think I could go visit him?" asked Doci.

"I am sure he would love a visit from a Frog Ponder. I will give you a letter to take to him. Now go to sleep. Your legs still need rest from your record-breaking run. Good night Doci."

The Windmill

The next morning Doci rolled off his log feeling the aches and pains of the race. Delayed Onset Muscle Soreness (DOMS) is not just for the Homo Sapiens. Even the endurance froggy athletes have to recover from extreme exercise. Ichy served up a delightful breakfast of pin cricket sautéed upon a sumptuous brisket of wood lice.

Ichy accompanied Doci down to the Confluence. Along the way a large number of departing animals stopped to shake Doci's hand and congratulate him on the new record.

"You are a celebrity now," smiled Ichy. "When greatness is thrust upon a frog, the real test of character is how you choose to treat those who loved you before the greatness."

Doci turned and gave Ichy a big hug. "I will never forget you Ichy. Thank you for letting me stay and thank you for the advice."

Ichy's face filled with smile and she patted Doci's arm. "Remember what you have learned my little friend from Frog Pond. When you have a dream, chase it with your whole being. Never let negative people and discouraging words dissuade you from living your **_VERY_** best life. Finally, know that believing is achieving so you might as well believe in something amazing."

Doci hugged his new friend goodbye and slipped into the river. Immediately the current swept Doci up and once more the adventure was afoot. The water felt cool and refreshing. Taut muscles relaxed and the aches and pains of the Citadel race seemed greatly diminished. Doci did not have to wait long before the Windmill came into sight. Ichy had said her brother lived in a wee cottage attached to the south side of the building.

A large barge filled with potatoes waited on the dock. The little frog had never seen so many vegetables. To him, the tower of spuds looked as formidable as the Citadel steps.

It was a Sunday morning and no one toiled in the fields. Ichy suggested this would be a good day to travel because LogFarm usually took his rest day pretty seriously. Doci had little trouble locating the cottage. A brass knocker in the form of a potato hung from the door. Extremely heavy, it took two hands and a great deal of huffing and puffing to lift it. Doci let the metal potato fall and a resonant boom echoed around him. He was just attempting to lift the knocker a second time when the door swung open.

In front of him stood a tall, middle-aged frog. Faded dungarees clung to sun-scorched skin. A straw hat tilted wildly on his head. Strategic holes cut in the crown allowed perky ears access to the heavens. "You must be Doci." LogFarm took the small hand in his own mighty maw and proceeded to shake it with the force of a jackhammer. "Oh, don't be so surprised. The whole valley knows who you are after this week's race. I couldn't be at the Citadel because of the potato harvest but I heard that a Northern Green Frog knocked off my sister's record. Hmm, the stories suggested you were a little bigger. So how is Logit these days, or should I say, how is Ichy?"

Doci smiled. From his pack he pulled out her letter and handed it to LogFarm. "She gave me this letter to give to you."

"Where are my manners?" LogFarm ushered Doci into the cottage. "I don't have company too often what with farming all year round. Mr. Badger is quite the task master."

"Do you like being a farmer?" asked Doci.

"Like it?" replied LogFarm, "I LOVE IT! If you want a piece of advice from me my friend, make sure that when you choose a career it is something that you are passionate about and something that gets you out of bed every morning. I'd go to work every day if Mr. Badger would let me. But he is one of those religious types and says the Sabbath is the day of rest and so today I rest."

"What do you love about potato farming?" asked Doci.

LogFarm shut his eyes and smiled. "What is not to love? Every day, I get to be outdoors in the fields. It is so exciting to take a little potato seedling and bury it in the ground. Then with careful watering and some nurturing that little seedling starts to sprout leaves. After a few months the whole field is green. But the real magic is what is happening underground. You see potatoes are root vegetables and they sprout beneath the soil. When the harvest day comes, we get to dig them up and the real fun begins. It is so exhilarating unearthing my little treasures. Every potato is different. Some are large, some are small, some are ugly, and some are beautiful. Some potatoes look like little trolls and some even look like froglets. Oh Doci, there is nothing I would rather do in all the world than farm potatoes."

Doci smiled, "you really do like your job. Has it always been that way for you?"

"Oh no," said LogFarm. At the very start it was very difficult. When I lived on my log in Frog Pond, I dreamed of exploring the world. I never saw myself as just a sitter. When the floods came and washed us over the dam it was like an answer to my prayers. Logit and me washed up on the island by the Citadel. On the first day there, I met Mister Badger who had just delivered a batch of potatoes to customers on the Confluence. When the barge pulled out, I stowed away and ended up following Badger to the Windmill. At first. he didn't want to hire me. He said that frogs are too small to be farmers. I begged him to give me a chance. Reluctantly, he let me have the far Northeast corner of his field on a trial run. The first week went so well and I think Mr. Badger was very impressed with my work ethic. He still wasn't convinced that a Frog could make it as a farmer. Then the accident happened and it changed everything."

"The accident?" asked Doci. "What was the accident?"

"Let's go for a walk and I can show you," said LogFarm.

The two frogs strolled across the field. The sun shone brightly and a cool easterly wind blew through the crop rows. LogFarm pointed out the different fields, crops, and potatoes in different stages of growth. In no time at all they arrived at a small ring of rocks which looked very much like an old well. The strange thing about the well was instead of an empty shaft in the ground it seemed completely full of earth.

"Here it is," said LogFarm proudly.

"What is it?" answered back Doci.

"This is where my life changed forever."

LogFarm loved a good story and Doci enjoyed hearing them. They sat down in the grass and LogFarm began his tale.

"I had only been working this field for five days when I went down with laryngitis. I completely lost my voice and couldn't even get out a simple croak let alone a conversation. It was a hot day and I came over to the well to get a drink of water. Little did I know but this well is dry and has no water. It didn't stop me from trying to wind myself down in the bucket. The rope was very old and frayed. Suddenly, it gave under my weight and I tumbled 100 feet down into the dark depths of the well shaft. Some of the other workers saw me fall and rushed to help me. Alas, the shaft was too dark and narrow. I lay on the bottom trying to call for help but I had no voice. I could hear the farmers up above talking. Then I heard Farmer Badger's loud voice. He called down into the well several times. His voice echoed so loudly it gave me a ringing headache. I remember it went quiet for several hours. Doci, I was so scared just lying there in the dark. Then it started raining only it didn't feel wet like water. Suddenly, I realized that it wasn't water at all. The farmers were throwing in soil. It seems they thought that no Frog could have survived such a fall. Mr. Badger was so sad and decided to fill in the well so no one else would have a similar accident. I lay there and watched shovelful after shovelful of dry earth come careening down the well shaft. At that moment Doci, I had to make a choice. I could have continued to lie there and given up on life. But no, I wanted to be a farmer and I was going to fight for my dream."

"What did you do? Doci asked.

"Well my young friend. I wriggled out of the broken bucket and shook off the dirt. Then I stood on top of the mound and started singing a little song. Every time a new lump of soil hit my head, I sang… 'Shake it Off and Step on Up.' For a whole hour, I sang the same song, 'Shake it Off and Step on Up.' Every time the soil hit me, I dug myself out and stepped a little higher. You can imagine the surprise when eventually the pile of soil got high enough to reach the top of the well, and there stood little LogFarm peering over the ledge. Oh, what a celebration party the old Badger threw. The story is almost as legendary as that of my sister being the first to conquer the Citadel." LogFarm let out a roar of laughter. "Since that day, I have worked very hard to learn as much as possible about potato farming. Farmer Badger says that I am the best potato farming Green Frog in all of the world. There is nothing like being the very best at something that you love to do."

The sun dipped beyond the horizon and in no time at all starlight replaced daylight. Doci felt captivated by the beauty of the stars. The two frogs sat in wicker rocking chairs out on the porch listening to the cicadas sing.

Doci sighed contentedly. "You know what LogFarm, you have a beautiful home and a wondrous life. I hope I can feel this happy when I grow up."

LogFarm chortled, "happiness is a choice little friend. Things don't make you happy, choices make you happy. The best choice of all is to smile every day, surround yourself with positive people, and commit 100% to something you care about. If you can remember those three things then you will find happiness wherever you lay your hat. Talking of laying down a hat, it is way past my bed-time. Those potatoes will not pick themselves. I have a date with a harrow at 4:30a.m. How about we get some good old shut eye? Tomorrow morning, I will send you across the river to meet my younger brother Logabin. He is an entrepreneur and the real brains of the family. Logabin runs a business, building yurts for all kinds of animals. I believe he named it 'Logabin's Cabins.'"

True to his word, LogFarm rose with the annoying cockerel. Doci, still fatigued from the race, slept on till noon. LogFarm came home for lunch and the two frogs sat and ate pickled weevils together on the porch.

At the boat dock, the two new friends said goodbye. LogFarm produced a small object from a pocket in his overalls. He unwrapped the cloth to reveal a potato. "Doci, I want you to take this with you. When you find that special place to lay your hat, I want you to plant it. Perhaps this can be one way to remember your adventure. Remember, never give up and choose to be happy."

Old Farmer Badger appeared beside them. "Hey partners. Did I understand that a friend of my friend needed a ferry across the river?"

LogFarm smiled, "Thank you Sir. Take good care of this one. He is a champion endurance athlete and world traveler." Doci grinned back and hopped up onto the gangplank.

"Thank you, LogFarm…Happy farming my friend!"

The Cabins

Logabin's Cabins stretched for miles in every direction. To a tiny frog from the Pond, a small city of log cabins was a real sight to behold. The community included small huts, medium sized yurts, large ranches, and colossal mansions. Even more remarkable than the structures were the residents of Logabin's metropolis. Snails, lizards, snakes, birds, goats, ponies, and even a rather odd, and out-of-place, penguin were residents of the community.

Logabin waited for the barge to pull up to the jetty. A dashing figure in a blue satin waistcoat with velvet breeches, Logabin looked every part the successful businessman. His expensive looking bowler hat seemed quite antithetical to his brother's straw boater. A pristine white shirt with a brightly colored red cravat topped off Logabin's wardrobe.

Doci hopped down the gangplank straight into the unexpected embrace of the eccentric real estate mogul. Logabin had extremely long arms and was almost a half-foot taller than Doci.

"Welcome to my little village Doci."

"How did you know I was coming to visit," asked Doci.

"You clearly made an impression with my brother LogFarm. He sent one of his favorite passenger pigeons across the river with a note. One of these days I am going to invent the telephone which will make communicating across the confluence much easier." Logabin smiled broadly. "Well Champion of the Citadel. Are you ready for a guided tour?"

Doci mirrored his host's excitement. "You bet Sir."

"Well, my carriage awaits so let's get going."

Doci looked over Logabin's shoulder. Two beautiful Shetland Ponies with long silver manes pawed the ground impatiently. A harness tied them into a small black carriage with red taffeta cushions. Doci's mouth gaped wider than the cheddar gorge. He had never seen a conveyance so enthralling.

Logabin seemed genuinely enamored at the reaction of his guest. Doci meet Apple and Strudel. They work for me in exchange for a log stable I built for them just last summer. Simply the very best employees any frog could ever ask for." Picking up the reins, Logabin gave them a little rustle. Immediately and in perfect unison the two ponies started down the road to town.

A large wooden sign hung across the road between two poles. It read in very large embossed letters – *'Logabin's Cabins.'* As they rolled through town Logabin gave Doci the grand tour. The layout stretched a veritable smorgasbord of structures and no two buildings looked the same.

"When I was a very small boy, I dreamt of building stuff," said Logabin. "I remember living on the log at Frog Pond staring at all the interesting trees and thinking what cool shapes I could construct given the chance. Then the flood arrived and washed me and my seven siblings down the river. This might be hard to believe, but I have never been a good swimmer. Several times I almost drowned but Logit and LogFarm swam beside me and kept me up above the water. Eventually we got separated somewhere around the Confluence." Logabin paused to wipe sweat from his brow with a silky handkerchief that magically appeared from his inside breast pocket. Secreting the hankie away, he continued. "I got washed up on a desolate sandbar a few hops down stream. The rains had stopped and the sun started to beat down with the fury of a cornered muskrat. I started to hop down the shore when to my horror I noticed thousands and thousands of wriggly worms littering the beach. There were so many that I could not take a step without stepping on one. You see, the pounding raindrops had brought them up out of the ground. Now the sun rose and the poor little blighters were literally baking to death."

    The elegant handkerchief once more arrived on the scene as Logabin dabbed the corners of his eyes. "Hundreds and thousands of little earthworms were literally dying that day. I looked up and I noticed a tiny raccoon not much older than three summers. He stood by the forest edge and seemed to be picking up the worms and throwing them into the woods. I stopped to watch mesmerized by the plucky dedication of this masked wonder. Again and again, he would stoop down and pick up handfuls of worms and hurl them into the woods. Finally, I could contain my curiosity no longer. I sidled up and asked him, 'what are you doing?'"

That little raccoon did not even pause to look at me but kept picking up the little wriggly fellas, sending them spiraling into the dark shady woods. While he worked, he said, "'these worms are dying in the sun, I am trying to get them back into the shade.'"

"Again, I looked around me and saw the thousands of poor souls languishing in the heat. I said to him, 'Sir, if you don't mind me stating the obvious, but there are gabbillions of worms out here, what difference can you possibly hope to make?' I will never forget his response."

"For a short moment he paused and looked down at me with his mesmeric brown eyes. His piercing eyes, gazed deeply into my soul, he threw another earthworm into the woods and said, 'I sure made a difference to that one.'"

"Immediately, I gathered up as many worms as my little webbed feet could hold, and joined the raccoon in saving as many as possible from the sun. Amazingly, other animals emerged from the woods and saw what we were doing. Our example seemed to motivate them to action. Soon all kinds of animals were helping to save the lives of the soil dwellers. A miracle it was for sure. However, despite all of our grandest efforts there were still many poor souls who lost their lives that day."

"I remember sitting down on the sand with Oscar after we had buried the departed."

"Who is Oscar?" interrupted Doci.

"Oh, Oscar is the kindly raccoon. Well, we sat there and talked for hours. I knew at that moment what my calling in life was. I would build log cabins and wooded homes for any animal that requested one. I started the very next day and built an elongated underground trailer for the earthworm colony. Oscar loved the idea and became my foreman. He still is my partner even today. For three years we have worked to take care of the woodland animals and so was born the little settlement of Logabin's Cabins. I am very proud to have my name on the signpost of town."

"What a remarkable story and what a truly inspirational accomplishment," stated Doci. "I hope I am able to touch as many lives as you have."

"Doci, my little hopper, sometimes we touch lives in very quiet and subtle ways but these ways make the biggest difference of all. You know what, you really must be introduced to my younger sister Logic. She is a school-teacher and a remarkable froggette. She has dedicated her whole entire life to making a difference in the lives of her students. Personally, I would not have the patience to handle all of those little ragamuffins, but she has an aptitude for it. She is so popular that we have had to enlarge her schoolhouse three times just in the last year because she gets so many students."

"I would love to meet her," said Doci. "You truly have a quite remarkable family."

"Why thank you Doci," replied Logabin. "I think they are pretty amazing myself. Every now and again we try to get together for a family reunion and reminisce about the good old days when all we used to do was sit on a log in Frog Pond. Life has certainly delivered us apples and we have done our very best to create delicious apple juice."

Logabin drew up to an ornate wooden cottage with a pretty manicured lawn and a crystalline fountain throwing up spouts of water. The structure was dwarfed by many of the surrounding structures but it clearly had been built with great love and care.

"Welcome to home sweet home," said Logabin. "Believe it or not I am a simple frog and did not see the need to be wasteful. This little place serves my needs adequately and there is plenty of room to entertain friends and family. Come on in and rest your weary legs. We can have a sumptuous dinner and I can take you up to visit Logic in the morning."

Logabin unhitched Apple and Strudel. The two ponies gracefully curtseyed and then headed down the road to their stables. Doci watched them go and shook his head in wonder. What a magical world he was seeing. He thought about his family still firmly rooted on their log on Frog Pond and felt a wave of homesickness sweep once more through him. One day he would return and tell them of all his adventures.

The Schoolhouse

The next morning, Doci had the honor of meeting Logabin's partner Oscar. The raccoon had astounding musculature and could carry a small tree on his back. Oscar visited with Logabin to discuss the architectural plans for an ice-skating rink. It seemed the one resident penguin had invited some of his relatives from Argentina to come live on the Confluence. These penguins were extreme hockey fans and were willing to pay big bucks to get a rink installed.

After the meeting, Apple and Strudel reappeared to escort the frogs up to the schoolhouse. Logabin continued to point out the sights and sounds of the city as they started on their way. Logabin literally knew every person in town by name and occupation. The ride to the schoolhouse took the best part of an hour. The building stood on the very edge of town. Tall turreted towers erupted from the four corners giving the edifice a fortress-looking aspect. Logabin seemed to read Doci's mind and interrupted his thoughts.

"It is definitely an unusual structure for a school," stated Logabin. "But be honest, if you were a young'un what would get you excited to go to school to learn math? A boring square cube, or a spectacular castle?"

Doci had to concede, his host definitely had a point. As the carriage pulled up to the front, a drawbridge crashed down in front of them. The portcullis rattled skyward and a riot of animal youth cascaded into the forecourt. Logabin pressed a button on the window and the roof of the buggy exploded in a cavalcade of fireworks and color. Magically, the streamers carried foil wrapped candies from the heavens. The school children bubbled with excitement as they leapt around the wagon snatching candy out of the air.

In the pupil's wake hopped a distinguished mistress frog with tree green robes flecked with brown. The headmistress rolled her eyes and shook her head. "My dear brother Logabin. You certainly know how to make an entrance and disrupt the school day. We of course are going to have to explain to all of the parents why we are sending their children home from class with cavities and sugar highs." Logic kissed her brother on the cheek.

Logabin beamed, "can't let you have all of the fun, can I?" he said. "Headmistress Logic let me introduce you to Master Doci the world record holder and champion of the Citadel."

"This little guy is what the big fuss was all about?" Logic extended her hand. "It seems the Northern Green Frog has established quite a name for itself in these parts what with Logit and now Doci conquering the old church steeple. Congratulations young man it really is a very impressive accomplishment. Under 300 stomps so they tell me."

Doci smiled uncomfortably. The young frog did not enjoy being the center of attention.

"So, to what honor do I owe this visit from the Mayor of the Cabins?" asked Logic.

"Well, Doci has an interest in tracking down all of our siblings from Frog Pond. He has this strange fascination for adventure. For some reason he wants to go to school when most children spend their whole lives trying to escape it."

Logic laughed good naturedly. "Well, Doci better have a death wish if he is going to hang out with our older brother." The siblings shared a knowing glance. "Logabin you can leave Doci in my capable hands. I will show him around the castle and then tomorrow, I will take him up to meet Logout."

"Thanks Sis that would be great." Logabin shook Doci's hand vigorously. "Now remember my friend, one small action one after the other leads to mighty big reactions that can sometimes change the world. I hope we will see each other again. You are always welcome to come stay at the Cabins when you are passing through the Confluence." Reaching inside his purple suit,

Logabin produced a little blue sack. Inside the sack there was a single silver nail.

"I just wanted you to remember your visit" said Logabin. "Wherever you go, I want you to know that you are capable of building in your life exactly what you want. The trick is to have the correct tools, a little education, and the determination to get started. I hope one day you will build your own house and use this nail to start the project. Now go visit the school. Oscar and I sure had a lot of fun building it. We even engineered some secret passageways that the children still have yet to find."

Logic rolled her eyes as she waddled back over the drawbridge and under the portcullis. Doci followed a few steps behind.

"Thank you for showing me around" he said. "I never had the opportunity to go to school. Papa I'llsi didn't think school to be that important. He would say the only good education is a good hard kick in the underpants."

Logic smiled, "a very progressive philosophy on the teaching arts, I'm sure. At our school we try to teach more than just discipline. We teach biology, letters, numbers, geography, communication arts, motivation, and happiness. Those are the core seven subjects that students need to master in order to graduate."

The school's internal structure mirrored the breathtaking architecture outside. Majestic stairways with golden balustrades connected the upper stories. The walls were painted in bright colorful hues and large windows let natural light flood the marble-tiled floors. Class rooms were larger than most churches to fit the hundreds of youthful animals that attended school daily. Desks were crafted in all shapes and sizes to accommodate the smallest snail and the largest grizzly bear.

One curious feature of the school, it didn't have any internal doors. This made traveling the hallways very easy. It also meant that the littlest animals did not have to circumvent large heavy doorways. Ms. Logic passed through an archway and Doci felt a momentary pause in his breathing.

Logic spread open her arms. "Welcome to the library."

Truly a spectacular room, bookshelves stretched from floor to ceiling in every direction. Doci had never before seen a single book let alone a whole library of them. "This is amazing," he said. "One day I am going to learn how to read."

Logic stopped in her tracks. "What? You mean that the world traveler does not know how to read? We can't have the Citadel Champion wandering around the Confluence illiterate." The headmistress crossed to a small shelf and pulled out a small hard-backed book. "Sit down at the table young frog."

Doci did as he was told and Logic shuffled in beside him. I know I promised to take you to meet Logout tomorrow, but first I must teach you how to read. The children are all on Harvest

Break for the week so I have plenty of time to teach you. What do you say?"

"Ma'am I don't know what to say. That is such a kind offer."

"Great then let's get started," said Logic.

True to her word, Mistress Logic spent eight hours a day for a week teaching Doci how to read. An exceptional and willing student, Doci learned quickly. After only one day of study, he had his letters down. By day two he had learned how to write them. By the third day he managed to make it through his first novel, 'See Frog Run.'

Student and teacher were taking a break between sessions on day four. Doci turned to Logic and said, "thank you for taking the time to teach me. You are simply wonderful and an amazing teacher. You are making my dreams come true."

Logic patted his arm. "Thank you, young man. I have not always been such a good teacher though. When I first started, I made many mistakes. I remember one of my first years in teaching. A sloth came to school one day. They have a reputation for being a little lazy and slow, so I didn't give him as much attention as the other students. The sloth also came with an itinerant family who worked seasonally in the blackberry patch. The blackberry season is quite short and so the sloths don't stay in school very long. Sadly, the sloth is often bottom of the economic chain in most communities. One day I asked the class to write a paper on what they wanted to be when they grew up. Simon was in that class. He came to school two days later and turned in his essay. He actually was a pretty good writer. He wrote about his dream to become a successful llama farmer. The essay had amazing detail about the size of his ranch, the number of llamas, the amount of money he would earn, and the hundreds of animals that would come to stay and visit the ranch. Well, after I read the paper, I felt like I had no choice but to give him a D. Part of the assignment was to write about a realistic goal. Simon was a sloth. This could be no realistic goal for an itinerant sloth. I gave him the opportunity to rewrite his term paper for a higher grade. He went home to think about it and came back the next day. He turned in his paper and told me that he and his father had a conversation that night. His papa told him that it was completely his decision to rewrite for a better grade or accept the teacher's grade and comments. Simon decided to keep the dream and keep the grade. Just a few weeks later the blackberry season ended and the sloth family moved on."

Logic dabbed her eyes with a handkerchief in a manner reminiscent of Logabin's penchant for hiding his emotions. After composing herself she continued her tale.

"Years passed by and the school got bigger. Every now and again we take the children on fun field trips. Logabin had heard that a llama farm had arrived in the valley. He suggested that we take the 4th years down there to stay the night and ride the llamas. We had a wonderful time at the ranch. Everyone learned so much about the animals from Peru. On the very last night we had all gathered in the main hall to say thank you to our host. He had been gone on a trip to the Andes to collect more llamas. Imagine my surprise when I saw the Head Rancher come through the door wearing cowboy boots and a fedora. You see the rancher was none other than Simon the Sloth. When he saw me, he rushed over and gave me the biggest hug. I couldn't believe my froggy eyes. He took my hand and led me very slowly over to a frame on the wall. There in the frame hung his school paper with a large red "D" in my handwriting. I remember sobbing in his arms for a long time. You see Doci, when I first started teaching, I was a 'Dreamstealer.' I learned a valuable lesson that day. It changed me as a teacher. From that moment on I made a commitment to never again steal away someone's dreams. Now I spend every day helping my students achieve their dreams no matter how big, small, or outrageous. Simon is a dear friend now and we take field trips to his llama farm at least twice a year."

Doci loved the story. "Ms. Logic, thank you for sharing your story. Thank you most of all for teaching me how to read and write. You are not a dream-stealer at all. I think you are a dream-weaver."

Logic reached over and patted her student's arm. "You are so very kind Doci. I wish all of my students learned as quickly as you do. Remember if you want to learn something new there are two important ingredients. One you have to ***WANT*** to learn. Two you have to be ***WILLING*** to ***COMMIT*** to learning. You my young Green Frog have a large helping of both.

By the end of the week, Doci could read everything Ms. Logic placed in front of him.

"I am so proud of you Doci. Now you will be able to go back and teach your family how to read and write." Doci felt again the familiar pangs of homesickness. Ms. Logic was right though, how fun would it be to sit down and teach We'llsi and You'llsi how to read.

Logic continued. "Doci you need to get a good night's sleep. Tomorrow Logout is coming down from the mountain to get you. Be prepared he is a little crazy. If you like adventure then you will love hanging out with crazy old Logout."

The Mountain

Standing outside the drawbridge, Doci admittedly felt a rush of nervousness. Certainly, he had experienced some big adventures, but some of the stories Logabin and Logic told suggested that a day with Logout could be the last spent in possession of one's own life.

Ms. Logic had asked the whole school to gather in the square for a special presentation. A small staging area had been set up and the headmistress stepped up to address the students. "Today, I am honored to present a special diploma." Taking a small metal canister, she popped off the top and extracted a small scroll of parchment. Unfurling it she read out aloud,

On the recommendation of the Faculty and by virtue of the authority vested in them the Trustees of the School has conferred upon Doci of Frog Pond the diploma of High School Graduate with all the honors and privileges pertaining to that accomplishment. In testimony

whereof, the seal of Mistress Logic are hereunto affixed this 10th day of July, 2022.

Doci hopped up the platform steps to accept his diploma. The student body cheered and clapped. Amid the applause a dark shadow swung across the square. High above the school a strange object circled. The wingspan was immense. With an almighty "whoop" the beast swooped toward the ground. Animals dived for cover as the peaceful gathering transformed into a riotous chaos. The winged aeronaut gathered speed and smashed headlong into the podium. The implosion sent carpentry flying everywhere. As the dust settled a single small figure emerged from the debris.

"It's alright, I am not injured. No harm done. I will live to fly another day." The strange frog hobbled out of the wreckage and tenderly stroked the fuselage of the flyer. "Although I am not sure Gertrude is going to fly again."

By now the student body had returned from their hiding places and nervously approached the stage. Ms. Logic crossed impatiently to stand between the masses and the mad pilot.

"Logout you are an idiot. What are you thinking coming here and endangering the lives of my sweet children?" She punched him on the arm.

Much to the children's joy, Logout acted like the punch had power and threw himself across the ground. The children roared with laughter. Logout was indeed a strange sight. On his head he wore bright pink goggles secured to an orange-cloth cap. Fluorescent shades of red, green, blue, yellow, and purple dotted his flying jacket and on his legs, he wore the ugliest puce colored bell bottoms Doci had ever before beheld.

"Logout, when you dig yourself off the pavement, please have the pleasure of meeting our friend Doci. You were just in time to destroy his graduation ceremony."

"Glad I didn't miss it. Sorry for being just a tad late and a little uncoordinated."

"Uncoordinated," fumed Logic, "you about killed the 1st-grade squirrels and you decimated the graduation platform."

Logout grinned, "that's okay, Logabin and that scamp Oscar will be able to fix it all up in a jiffy."

Logout extended a paw of greeting to Doci. "So nice to meet you, my friend. It is an honor to meet a fellow legend. I happened to watch some of your epic race at the Citadel. I used to want to enter the race myself, but I have big bunions on my heel and all those steps just look like hell for bunions."

Doci smiled, Logout was definitely a little eccentric but he sure did have a fun sense of humor.

"So, headmistress can I have permission to take your newest student on an adventure?" asked Logout.

"Only if you promise to bring him home in one piece," announced Logic.

"No guarantees, but I will most surely do my best," said Logout. "Can you see if Logabin can fix my glider when he shows up to fix the stage?"

"Logout you are incorrigible." Logic gave her brother a big hug then turned to Doci.

"Doci thank you for coming to visit my school. Thank you for being a wonderful student and affording me the opportunity to teach you how to read. It has been a wonderful honor. Please accept this diploma as a memory of our time together." Logic presented the silver tube to Doci and he placed it carefully in his little knapsack.

"Thank you, Ms. Logic. I don't know what to say."

"Then say nothing young man. Oh, and don't get killed while you are out playing with my crazy brother."

Doci watched his new friend return to school across the drawbridge with five hundred woodland creatures in tow. Doci shook his head, what a truly remarkable frog Logic was.

"Ready to get going Frog Ponder?" asked Logout.

"Sure," he replied. "Where are we going?"

"That my friend is a big surprise," replied Logout. "The first part is a bit of a hike so we better get going."

The two frogs set off across the playground then turned west into the woods. In a short hour of hiking, the sound of roaring started to increase in crescendo. Water droplets spackled Doci's head. A majestic waterfall materialized right in front of them. Eighty feet of gushing flow pulsed over a hanging rockface. Far below, a mist of spray evidenced the fluid receptacle for the pouring thunder.

Logout smiled manically at Mother Nature's violent portrait. "This reminds me of a great story," he said. "Once upon a time there was a beloved king who ruled wisely. A connoisseur of the arts, he issued a competition for an artist who could paint a portrait of peace. Artists came from miles around to enter the competition. Finally, the king settled on two finalists. The first picture depicted a calm lake surrounded by majestic green forests and snow-capped mountains. The sun shone down and white fluffy clouds coasted through an azure blue sky. The second finalist illustrated rugged and bare mountains with a violent waterfall careening down from jagged peaks. To all observers the first picture seemed to be the obvious winner. However, the king surprised everyone by selecting the waterfall portrait. When asked about his decision, the king pointed to a single detail. Behind the waterfall, a small bird had constructed its nest within the confines of a scraggly bush. The king spoke boldly, 'peace is not about being in the absence of noise, trials, loudness, and conflict. True peace is the ability to find calm amidst the chaos of everyday life."

Logout smiled, "I come up here to escape the world and find peace and solitude and to plan my next big adventure."

"Next adventure? Do you have something in mind?" Doci shuffled nervously away from the cliff edge.

"Life is worth living to the fullest my friend," Logout yelled to be heard above the deafening roar of the falls. "Too many people are just out there **EXISTING** and clock-watching. We should be **LIVING** and taking advantage of every second. You know us frogs only get 10-12 years at most. Those two-legged giants that wander around in the cities get 9 or 10 times that but they are the worst "Existers" of all."

Logout continued up the trail and beckoned for Doci to follow. A few turns later the two frogs found themselves on a rocky ledge directly above the raging waterfall. A small bench with a wooden trunk beneath it greeted the travelers.

"I have been waiting for a long time to challenge the Falls," said Logout. "In truth it gets a little lonesome having big adventures all by myself. I have been waiting for a friend with some spirit to try something really fun."

Doci shook his head. "Oh, Logout I am not very good at heights."

Logout grinned broadly. "You handled the heights at the Citadel just fine. I promise going down is much easier than climbing up." The little frog pulled out the wooden trunk and threw back the latch. Pulling two bright orange jumpsuits out of the chest he proclaimed proudly, "I designed these myself. I was watching flying squirrels jump from the tree canopy. I thought to myself, I could make a suit that lets me glide like that." With a rapturous grin across his face, Logout held up his creation. "I call it a Squirfruit on account of the squirrels who gave me the motivation and the fact it makes you look like a Tangerine when you wear it."

Logout threw Doci a squirfruit and with fearful reluctance, Doci pulled it on. Surprisingly comfortable, the suit had meshy fabric that extended from the gloves to the ankles. Logout extended his arms and flapped. The wings rippled as they caught the air and water droplets coming off the Falls. "Here you might need this." Logout threw Doci an orange helmet made out of an acorn cup. "Just in case," he said.

The two frogs inched toward the precipitous ledge and peered over. Sunshine threaded its way through the mountains and bounced a spectrum of rainbows off the spiraling water. Logout yelled loudly to make himself heard above the crashing water. "On three, we are going to jump off the edge. Extend your arms and the suit will make you glide. If you want to go faster close your arms. If you want to go slower open your arms wide again." Logout pointed his spindly arm toward some fields in the far distance. Our goal is to squirfruit down the falls, then jettison out the bottom of the canyon into the cornfields. The farmers are baling hay and there are plenty of haystacks to land in."

"To land in?" Doci questioned incredulously. "You mean, you expect me to jump off this ledge, dive through a waterfall, pull up before crashing into the rocks below, fly over the river, across the field, and land in a haystack?"

"Yep, let's go."

Before Doci knew what was happening, Logout yanked him off the ledge and the two frogs were in tandem freefall. Doci tried running but no ground gave him purchase – only empty air.

"Spread your wings," shouted Logout as he let go of Doci. Doci extended his arms and immediately he felt himself slow.

"I'm flying," he thought. "I'm flying." Doci laughed manically as he followed Logout down the Falls. The adventurer's flight took him to the edge of the falls. Water droplets clipped the acorn helmet and doused the meshy wings. Tiny holes in the squirfruit let water pass freely through the arm panels and soon the two frogs found themselves soaring chaotically through the waterfall on a spiraling descent to the far river gorge below.

    Doci suddenly forgot to be afraid. Staying in the moment, he focused his attention on the task at hand. The river below surged to meet them. Logout was in a full dive and at the last second pulled his head up and stretched forth his meshy arms. The squirfruit caught the updraft and carried him across the river into the fields. Doci, pulled up a little earlier but still caught an updraft that sailed him clear of the jagged rocks lining the river. He watched as Logout barreled into a four-foot haystack. Doci looked wildly around for his landing pit. Alas, he found himself too high. Altering his flight path, he headed for the last haybale in the field. He overshot his mark and careened into a tree skirting the field. Twigs, leaves, and branches whipped his little green face. Orange material tore as the little frog pummeled tree bark. Doci shut his eyes and let nature take over. Seconds later, he stopped moving. Opening his eyes, he saw his legs dangling hopelessly beneath him and a large tree branch perforating his right wing. The perforation probably saved his life.

Doci quickly evaluated his situation. "Well, I am alive, I can wiggle all of my fingers and toes, nothing seems to be broken, but I am stuck up in this tree with no way to get down."

Below, an orange squirfruit appeared. Logout jumped ecstatically up and down. "Wasn't that ***AWESOME!*** I really only gave that a 50% chance of success. Epic! How are you doing up there Doci? I guess we should get you down."

"You think?" stated Doci not altogether politely. "Any ideas?"

"Sure, just wiggle out of the suit and I will catch you."

"You will catch me?" stated Doci with a heavy sense of foreboding.

"Trust me," threw back Logout.

Doci groaned, "okay here goes." He shimmied his legs out of the suit. Just as he tried to extricate an arm the suit fractured and Doci plunged groundwards. He landed in a big mess of shredded squirfruit and excitable Logout.

Logout definitely cushioned the fall but Doci bopped his head on the descent.

"That's a nasty bump you have on your head. Good job we are close to my sister's house. She can get that little scrape healed up right quick."

Logout, put his arm around Doci and together the adventurers headed down a little pathway into the woods.

The Hospital

White walls with multiple little windows popped into view. A large red cross had been painted on the front door of the building. The hospital stood alone in the middle of the glade. Logout boisterously bonked on the postern. A scurry of little feet and the door swung open. A wiry frog with steely-rimmed spectacles regarded the motley duo.

"Oh Logout, what have you been up to now?"

"Hi Doc," Logout carried Doci into the hospital. "I'm fine but my good friend Doci here got a bump on his head."

"Lay him down on the table and let me take a look at him." LogDoc inspected the wound and dabbed some gauze and warm water to clear up the matted blood. She then took out a small jar of putrid smelling ointment and smeared it all over the wound. Then artfully, she wound several bandages around Doci's rather more bulbous than usual head.

"There you are, all done," said Doc. "Although, I would like to keep you here for a day or two for observation." Doc leaned in and whispered, "and to keep you safe from my brother's next hair-brained scheme."

LogDoc turned to Logout. "So, what mental escapade did you attempt this time?"

"Sis, you should have seen us. We squirrafruited off of Legend Falls."

LogDoc shook her head. "You are a fruit and nut case Logout. One day, I am not going to be there to bandage you up and then what are you going to do?"

Logout smiled widely. "But think about all the business I bring you."

LogDoc bustled her brother out the door. "Go make yourself useful and help the nurses stock the supply cabinets."

Logout grinned at Doci as he allowed himself to be frog-handled out the door. "See you later Doci. You will love the hospital food." Logout contorted his face in pretend distress and disappeared down the hallway.

LogDoc shut the door and came back to sit beside her patient. "I love my brother but his penchant for adventure is going to put HIM in the hospital one of these days." The doctor checked Doci's dressings. "I can't be mad at him though. Logout has one of the biggest hearts in all the woodland. You know he worked for weeks without a break to build this hospital after the floods. He also saved my life."

Doci loved a good story. "I would love to hear your story. Your family is the most fascinating group of frogs I have ever before met."

LogDoc patted Doci's hand. "That is very sweet of you to say." The doctor took off her little stethoscope and settled into a chair.

"When our family was washed away over the Beaver Dam, we were all separated. As you know already, most of us ended up around the Confluence. I got caught up in the current and fought for hours to get out of the surge. I remember seeing a lot of lights and hearing lots of noise. Suddenly, a large net fished me out of the storm drain. One of those big-legs you sometimes see wandering around carried me into a huge building. It turns out she was a medical intern. She kept me by the window in her room in a large terrarium on her desk. Every day she sat by the window reading medical textbooks and looking at videos on the computer. I learned a lot from watching those programs and reading over her shoulder. Then one day, I got very scared. You see, the chapter she had open detailed how to do a frog dissection. Suddenly, I realized that I was not a pet but rather a future homework assignment. I was trapped. I started flashing SOS in morse code by reflecting sunlight off the building across the road." A single tear came to

LogDoc's eye and peeled down her cheek. "Then suddenly, he was there."

"Who was there?" blurted out Doci who was enthralled by the story.

"Logout! He swung through the open window on the back of an eagle and knocked the terrarium upside down. Then he grabbed me, pulled me up beside him and off we flew. I have never been so scared in all my days. How he found me I will never know."

Doci looked dumbfounded. "He flew in on the back of an eagle?"

"Oh, that is another really cool part of our family story. You will have to meet Logjam to hear about how Logout befriended the eagles."

"Who is Logjam?" inquired Doci.

LogDoc smiled. "You will love Logjam, she is the youngest of my siblings and the most accomplished pâtissier in all of the shire. Now rest for a little while and we can talk more later."

*****

For the next few days, Doci explored the little woodland hospital. Every brick and beam exuded a polished serenity. Despite injury, illness, and disease walking through the door, a harmonic optimism resonated through the walls. Laughter, music, excitable chatter, and brightly colored flowers flowed through the healing spaces. LogDoc and her staff welcomed all manner of forest creature with an exuberant joyful spirit.

Toward the end of the third day, Doci joined LogDoc and Logout for dinner on the 1st floor patio. The autumn sun bowed reverently below the horizon bathing the glade in soft bronzing light. Logout stretched languidly in his chair a mischievous squint in his eye. "Ready for another adventure Doci?"

LogDoc kicked her brother under the table. "I think our guest from Frog Pond is due a moment of respite." Turning to Doci, the doctor spoke softly. "Perhaps a visit with Logjam will suit? Here we heal the physical ailments and maladies. My sister's food and spirit, has the power to promote emotional and spiritual healing."

"I would very much like to visit your sister. Your family is incredible." Doci rubbed his head with a webbed thumb. "Before I go, I have to ask, how on earth did Logout find you after the flood?"

The amphibious siblings smiled at one another. Logout spoke first, "me and Doc are twins and we have always had a tight bond. When we were tadpoles, we used to finish one another's sentences. It's like we have built in radar for finding one another. My brothers and sisters feared the worst, but Doc here is a Violet Jessop and I knew I'd find her."

Doci looked confused, "what is a Violet Jessop?"

LogDoc smiled, "Violet Jessop is a story of legends among the tall-two-legs. Their history books call her the "Queen of Sinking Ships" or "Miss Unsinkable." Violet was a medic just like me. She served as a maritime stewardess and nurse aboard some very large ships. In 1911, she was on the RMS Olympic when it collided with the British warship HMS Hawke. Then in 1912, she took a post on the RMS Titanic. On April 14th, it struck an iceberg and began to sink. Violet was ordered into Lifeboat 16 and told to hold a baby that had been separated from its mother. The little 5-month old boy was reunited with his mother on board the Carpathia. Violet survived the sinking of the Titanic and returned to England."

LogDoc took a sip of chamomile tea and continued. "During World War I, Violet took a position with the British Red Cross and served on the hospital ship the HMHS Britannic, the younger sister ship of the Titanic. On the morning of November 21, 1916, the Britannic ran into a German mine and sank into the Aegean Sea. Violet Jessop made it into a lifeboat but had to jump into the ocean when the ship's propellers started to shred the lifeboats. Somehow, Violet survived even after sustaining a significant head trauma."

"You would think three sinkings would have scared her away from nursing on the ocean. Nope, she continued as a medical steward for the Red Star Line and sailed twice around the world on the Belgenland before finally retiring 35 years later."

Logout spoke up, "Doci you might be wondering why the story of Violet Jessop is so important to my sister?"

Doci nodded, he did in fact have to admit to a curiosity on this topic.

LogDoc spoke quietly, "well during my stay with the medical students, I got to learn a lot about the young woman doctor who saved me from the storm drain. It turns out her name is Mary Thomas, the great-great-great niece of Alex "Assed" Thomas, the little boy whom Violet Jessop rescued from the sinking Titanic. So just as Violet saved Alex, Mary in a way saved me. I feel it falls now upon me to help others. It is a way to pass it forward."

Logout nodded. "I agree with my sister. In so many ways we are all connected. Helping others is just one opportunity to move the world forward." The spindly older frog pushed a bowl of waxworms toward his guest. "Eat up, tomorrow you meet my sister and her eagles."

The Eyrie

Nothing could have prepared Doci for his first glimpse of the EYRIE. In the depths of pre-dawn morning, Logout and Doci crept out of the hospital. The kindly bunny rabbit orderlies had prepared a packed lunch. It had been an exciting adventure climbing the mountain. A few minutes into the hike, Logout stopped and whistled. A beautiful forest pony with a sleek grey coat appeared like magic from the dark wooded canopy.

"Doci, this is my friend Emma. She has agreed to take us up the mountain. A hike that for us could take weeks will only take Emma a couple of hours. She is the fastest forest pony in the land and no one is as sure-footed on the mountain trail as her."

Emma whinnied and tossed her head in delight at hearing the compliment. The pony dipped her head towards the ground and Logout bounced up the white blaze that ran from ear to nose. Doci followed suit and the two frogs settled comfortably into Emma's fluffy main.

Spangles of sunbeam reflected off the canyon as Emma slowed. Logout prodded Doci awake. There in front of them stretched the 'Eyrie.'

Concentric levels of rock and stone combined to form a majestic city of terraces. Large nests spread themselves opulently atop spires of granite. High in the air circled eagles with the wingspans of small airplanes. Doci felt the cooler air catch in his throat. "It is beautiful," he whispered.

Emma trotted up to a large wooden gate blocking the trail. A balding ferret holding a kitchen fork poked his head over the balustrade.

"Who goes there?" he shouted.

"Hi Isaac, it is only Logout and his friend Doci. We are here to seek an audience with the Royal Cheffette."

Isaac hit a small bell and the gate slowly turned inward. "Great to see you friend Logout. There is talk that two strange orange birds are flying around the waterfall. You don't know anything about that do you?"

Logout winked at Doci. "Nope, haven't seen any orange birds but I will keep a look out for them."

Isaac pointed to some steps off to the right of a spacious courtyard. "Logjam is in the kitchen trying to concoct a new culinary delight for his majesty's birthday. She will be excited to see you."

Doci and Logout jumped to the ground and thanked Emma. Isaac ferreted out an apple from his pocket. "Good girl Emma. Thank you for bringing the froggies up. I am sure we can find someone to ferry them back down the valley."

Isaac winked at Logout. Logout beamed with that look of excitement that Doci recalled all too well when his friend pushed him off the waterfall.

A long spiral of stone steps descended ahead. Mouth-watering aromas wafted upwards. The smells erupted a cavalcade of olfactory emotion. Doci felt his stomach grumble in concert with the fruity scent. He momentarily stopped on the stairs to take a deep breath. Logout, not paying attention, barreled into him from behind. Doci lost his feet and tumbled in an accelerating mess of arms and legs. Before he could slow himself, he slammed into a warm body. The collision sent the two of them careening into a table of fruits, jams, and pies.

Doci lay on the floor stunned, his spindly legs entwined in the spindly arms of another frog. Sitting up he looked directly into the most beautiful eyes he had ever seen. Only, those beautiful eyes were none too pleased about the unceremonious descent into bakery chaos. A bowl of emulsified peaches slid off the table top and landed plum on Doci's head. The other frog's lips began to twitch uncontrollably. Soon, the room filled with raucous giggles and rapturous laughter.

Logout arrived at the foot of the stairs. He regarded for a moment the scene and burst into side-stich hiccup-ing guffaws. Doci and Logjam sat opposite each other in various states of contortion. Doci had a bowl of fresh peaches on his head and various red and purple jams smeared across his cheek. Logjam was barely recognizable covered in custard cream, pineapple jelly, and golden molasses.

Doci staggered to his feet and extended a hand. Logjam scooped a handful of peach custard from Doci's head and put it to her lips.

"Delicious," she exclaimed. "I think we have found the King's birthday surprise. I would never have thought to mix peaches, pineapples, custard, molasses, and gooseberries." Logjam looked at Doci and threw her arms around the surprised frog. "Thank you so much for helping me find this recipe."

"My pleasure," Doci stammered.

Logout hooted with laughter. "Hi little sister, let me introduce you to squirsuit flyer and

Citadel step-climbing champion, Doci of Frog Pond."

Getting back to her feet, Logjam smiled sweetly and extended a hand. "It is a pleasure. Welcome to the Royal Kitchens of the Eagle Eyrie."

Logjam put two fingers in her mouth and whistled. Instantly, four small stoats appeared from flaps in the outer wall. Turning to a weasel in a pink frilly overall she said, "Bessy, could you and your sisters help me clean the kitchen while I go bathe and find a new apron?"

The tiny stoats went straight to work with little mops, buckets, and brushes. The three frogs exited stage right and a small tunnel took them to a cave with a pool of crystal water. Doci dipped his toe in the water. Warm!

Seeing his surprised expression, Logjam explained, "the waters on the mountain are warmed by hot springs. The eagles say the mountain is actually a sleeping volcano. They love it up here because even when the winds are howling, the springs and nests are kept warm and cozy because of the geothermals."

The three frogs hopped into the water to clean themselves and relax.

Logjam, smiled. "Have you heard the story about the frog in hot water?"

Doci shook his head.

"Well one day, a French villainous cook decided he would cook up some frog legs for his king. The problem was he had no frogs. One day he stood in the kitchen stirring a pot of boiling water. A frog jumped on the window ledge. The cook tried to trick the frog and said, come jump in my warm swimming pool. The frog jumped into the pot but the water burned his skin and he jumped right back out and ran away. The cook cursed his luck but changed his strategy. He took the pot off the heat and waited. Two other frogs hopped by and he invited them to partake in his nice warm pool. Wanting to rest from their hard day, they jumped into the pot and lounged. Little-by-little, the chef raised the heat on the stove. The two frogs did not notice the incremental raising of the temperature until it was too late. They had grown so comfortable that they didn't notice the water boiling them. When they passed out, the king ended up with frogs-legs for dinner."

Doci and Logout looked at Logjam aghast. "Sister, that is a horrible story. It is a story fit for Halloween not a King's birthday feast."

Logjam laughed out loud. "Actually, it is more about the lesson. Sometimes we can grow too comfortable doing the same thing day-in-and-day-out. Before you know it, you might have missed an opportunity to do something else."

"Do you not like cooking for the Eyrie?" asked Doci.

"I love being the King's Pastry Chef, and boy do those eagles love their cakes. I just wonder if I should be doing something else."

Doci wrinkled his nose from the faint smell of sulfur pervading the cave. "How does a frog come to be the head chef for an eagle king?"

Logjam grinned at her brother who smiled back. "That is a really cool tale." Logjam settled her shoulders against the edge of the pool, sighed and started her story.

"When the big rains came, we were not ready for the swell that washed us over the Beaver Dam. All eight of us hung on desperately as our logs hurtled over the dam and into the river. We were all separated quickly." Logjam paused briefly. "I was the youngest and had never been away from my family. Suddenly, they were gone and I found myself all alone on the river. I grabbed a lily pad and held on for dear life. Muddy water filled with branches, twigs, and even complete trees flowed downstream. I saw many animals caught up in the flood." Tears came to Logjam's eyes. "So many of our woodland friends did not make it."

"After many hours of being tossed around, I must have fallen asleep. When I woke up, I didn't know where I was. Everything looked so strange and unfamiliar. For a moment, I even thought I might have died and gone to a strange Frog Heaven. I lay in the reeds for several days not daring to move."

"Moma had taught me all about different berries, roots, and grasses. I knew what I could eat and what I should stay away from. At night time, I crept out from my hiding place in the bulrushes to eat. One of these nights, I came upon a very strange sight."

"For a few days, I had heard a painful squawk coming from the river edge. It sounded so sorrowful. This night, I came face-to-face with the source of the squawk. A small eagle lay in the muddy quagmire. One wing was completely submerged in the river and the other flapped uselessly at its side. The bird could not raise his head. A fisherman's net had got entangled around the eagle's neck and most of the net had been pinned by a sharp tree beneath the water's surface." Logjam shut her eyes as she recaptured the image of the trapped eagle.

"I felt so bad for the injured eagle. I wanted to help but what could a little frog do. I conjured up some courage and tried to talk to the bird. I said, 'Hello, Mr. Eagle, I see that you are tangled up. Can I try and help you?' Well, that eagle just looked at me through his squinting right eye. His beak completely latched shut because of the net.

I dove into the river and saw that the net snagged on a heavy branch. I worked for hours beneath the surface trying to untangle the net. By nightfall, I had managed to loosen it enough so that the eagle could open his beak and breathe easier.

I found out that his name was Artur. He had been flying high above the storm. Eagles are not bothered by a little rain and wind. Unfortunately, he got a little disorientated and when he flew lower a wind gust caught him and threw him into the river. His beak got tangled in a net and when he tried to free himself his neck and talons got tangled up too.

Artur had not eaten in several days so I explored the riverside and found food for him to eat. There were blackberries, wild raspberries, boysenberries, crab apples, and all kinds of mushrooms. The rains had also brought out an ample supply of worms and grubs.

For the next few days, I worked around the clock to free Artur from the net and collect food. Finally, the net below the surface fell away and Artur managed to shake the net from his head. Unfortunately, the right wing had many tears and Artur could not fly. I cleaned the mud off his wings, and brought honey from the forest. I remember GrandMaFrog teaching me that honey could heal all kinds of things.

Artur loved my food and I loved his stories. He shared about his home, the Eyrie, and how all the eagles lived together in a community on top of a mountain. He told me that his dad was King of the Eyrie. He also promised me that once he could fly, he would take me to the Eyrie so I could see it for myself.

After a few weeks, Artur grew stronger. He began to stretch and flap his wings. One morning I brought him an elderberry jam wafer. Artur was particularly partial to my jams.

He said to me, 'from now on I will call you Logjam. Today, I am ready to try flying.'

Artur invited me to get on his back and then with two downbeats of his wings, we were soaring above the bulrushes. I had never experienced such exhilaration. The view from the clouds is incredible. I didn't have time to be scared, I was too busy falling in love with flying.

Artur and I flew up the river and over the woods. Soon the mountains came into view. Artur sung a beautiful song and his voice suddenly joined with a hundred other eagles that swooped from the peaks. Artur enjoyed a beautiful reunion with his father King Egron and they asked me to stay on as the Royal Pastry Chef.

King Egron was so very grateful for me helping save his son. He immediately sent out search parties for my siblings. One of those search parties found Logout who had walked for days up and down the river looking for me. Logout came and lived at the Eyrie for a while. The eagles are so kind. Artur and Logout are best friends and eventually they found LogDoc locked up in a transparent box in the city. They rescued LogDoc and now my sister runs the hospital down in the forest. Thanks to the eagles, and Logout, I now know where all of my seven siblings are. We have been talking about a reunion of sorts sometime soon."

Doci, shook his head in bewilderment. "What a crazy story."

"I know, who would have thought me a Royal Pastry Chef?" answered back Logjam.

Doci laughed, "what else did you learn from living with the eagles?"

Logjam, pursed her lips for a few seconds. "Eagles are amazing creatures. They have phenomenal vision and can spot a rabbit over two miles away. I have also watched them be fearless hunters. The eagles are not scared of any creature in the woodland and most animals respect the eagle. They are tenacious protectors and defenders of their young. The eagles defend their homes and are extremely loyal to one another. The eagles are also not scared of heights. They can fly above 10,000 feet in the high mountains. I have never seen an eagle shirk a challenge. Their determination is truly an inspiration. But my favorite quality of the eagles is how much they care for the little ones."

Doci smiled, "it sure sounds like you have learned a lot from living with the eagles."

Logjam nodded. "But perhaps the most important thing I learned was, no matter how small you are you can always make a difference in someone or something much larger than you."

"Amen sister," croaked Logout. "Now, how about we get out of this bathtub and go eat some pie?"

****

That night Doci was a guest of honor at King Egron's birthday party. Everyone had a good giggle when Logjam told the story of how she concocted the king's new dish – Pineapple Custard with Gooseberry Molassess.

Doci found himself experiencing a strange emotion throughout the evening. He reflected on his adventure and smiled. Is this happiness he thought to himself?

He noticed Logout and Artur in deep conversation towards the end of the night. Disengaging from the chat, Logout stepped towards Doci.

"Well, that is all settled."

"What is settled?" inquired Doci.

"Artur has agreed to accompany us on a little journey."

"Journey?" Doci shuffled with excitable discomfort. "What kind of a journey?"

Logout smiled good naturedly. "Oh, this is going to be a good one. I think you will enjoy it immensely. Of course, we do have to visit one more of my siblings before we begin."

The Workshop

Flying is not something frogs are designed to do. Squirfruiting had done little to improve Doci's fear of heights. Now, here he was soaring through the rooftops of the forest on the back of an eagle. Doci sat upon a rudimentary soft saddle constructed out of compacted feathers and tree cotton. Logout sat at the front, Logjam in the middle and Doci held on fearfully at the back. The eagle's wings beat powerfully creating a mesmeric muffled syncopation with every downbeat. Only a few minutes passed since departing the Eyrie, it felt like hours for Doci and the circulation in his legs stalled from holding on so tight.

Artur, Prince of the Eagles, flew carefully and with precision, conscious of the precious cargo transported between his wings. Logout prodded Artur gently and pointed downwards. Doci stole a glance over his shoulder. On the ground below stretched what looked like an army of animals. Like a Roman legion preparing for battle, the figures seemed to await the command to advance.

Artur swooped into a clearing. Primary and secondary feathers contorted in different angles slowing the passage toward the ground. Long dark talons extended to find purchase on a nearby mossy knoll. Doci expected a big bang or a large bump. When he opened his eyes, Artur's beady eye regarded him with sympathetic mirth. Doci whispered "thank you" and slid down the wing to stand alongside his quickly disembarked companions.

Doci looked around awestruck. Mouth agape, the little frog started walking toward the army. He stopped at the first soldier. A tall beaver stood at attention a whole three feet taller than Doci. The beaver held a fierce looking lance in his right hand and a massive shield in the left. Long gauntlets extended down sinewed arms and intricate armor hung tightly on muscular appendages. On top of the beaver's head, a conical helmet with a feathery blue plume topped off the majesty of the uniform. Next in line stood a lanky weasel similarly attired and standing to attention. Doci continued down the line. Every manner of woodland creature stood patiently dressed in the same precise regalia. Every single creature artistically made of wood.

Logout stepped up to join Doci. "Have you ever seen anything like this?"

Doci stammered, "It is one of the most marvelous things I have ever seen. How many of them are there?"

Logout smiled, "at last count, I think Logger's army included 996 animals."

"996 carved sculptures?" Doci repeated the number as if somehow it would make more sense and become more believable if he said it out loud."

Logjam spoke up. "Some of us bake cookies, some of us dive off cliff-faces, some of us build houses, some of us teach classes, some of us farm the fields, and some of us bandage wounds. Logger carves wood."

Doci shook his head in wonder as he moved up and down the rows of soldiers studying the quality of the craftsmanship. "These are truly wonderful. I have never seen anything more magical."

Logout laughed. "Great, now Logger is never going to get that big head of his out of the woodshop."

Logjam laughed. "Let's go say hello to Mister Eccentric." She led the boys through the wooden statues. After a few minutes of walking, an old derelict barn came into view.

Shouting loudly, Logout yelled "you would think a master craftsmen would take more pride in the outside of his workshop."

The door opened and a lively frog in lime-green overalls walked towards them. "Brother it is the inside that is so much more precious than the outside."

Logjam disengaged from the group and threw her arms around Logger.

"I see they have let you escape the kitchens." Logger kissed his sister on the cheek. "I hope those emperors of the sky don't go hungry in your absence."

Logger stepped toward Doci. "Ah, this must be the traveler from Frog Pond." The woodcarver extended his hand. Doci grasped it and shook it vigorously.

Immediately, Logger let out a howl of pain. Doci pulled reactively away and looked down in his hand. There in his webbed fingers hung a bloody arm. Logger screamed in more pain. Doci dropped the severed arm on the grass bewildered, his heart in his throat.

Suddenly, Logger began to bellow with laughter. Doci struggled to follow the chaos. Logger pulled up his sleeve revealing a perfectly good arm. He picked up the wooden arm that Doci had dropped. "Just kidding with you."

Logout thumped Doci on the back. "I should have told you Logger is a trickster. I can't tell you how many times I have fallen for the "severed arm hoax."

Doci's heart still thumped a million beats a minute. "But it looked so real?"

Logjam sympathetically patted Doci on the head. "Yes, that was a particularly rude way to greet a visitor." She shot an annoyed glance toward Logger who looked down with a modicum of embarrassment.

"But I do have a wonderful surprise," bantered back Logger. Logout gave me the idea and I think it will work." He moved toward the workshop.

Inside, the barn was a cavern of sculptures at varying stages of completion.

Doci asked, "how did you get the idea for carving an army? It really is a remarkable creation. You are so talented."

Logger blushed a green-crimson. "Well, there is a bit of an interesting story there. When we got washed over the dam many years ago, I ended up in a tin can. The river raged and I kept getting pulled under. It was exhausting fighting the debris in the flood. Finally, I managed to pull myself up into a small dumpster floating downstream. I settled in to ride the storm out. At the bottom of the metal box hiding amongst the trash, I found a magazine. The booklet was grimy with a yellow cover and had a title – 'National Geographic.' Mama and Papa had taught us older kids to read. So, I spent the next few hours reading the April 1978 issue. On the front cover there was a picture of these life-size terracotta soldiers. It seems like a farmer digging a well in 1974, accidentally came across a clay head. They excavated the land and discovered a tomb built by the first emperor of China. Qin Shi Huangdi commissioned over 10,000 life-size warriors in full battle armor to be molded. Each warrior is distinctively different with hairstyle, clothing, facial features, and poses. When he died, he had them buried in the ground so that he would have an army in the after-life. I thought this idea to build an army was really cool. Eventually, I got washed up here. The workshop barn already had been abandoned. I spruced it up a little and started carving. My hope is that others will be inspired by our own wooden army and want to engage in the arts."

Logjam tenderly squeezed her brother's arm. "Tell Doci, the real reason you built your wooden army."

Logger's eyes glazed over for a moment. "When the floods came to Frog Pond, we were not ready. So many of our woodland friends perished in the Great Flood. This is my way of honoring all of our friends that passed that day. Also, the last thing I heard Papa say before we got whisked away was, "Make me Proud Son." I will never forget those words. I hope that he is looking down from Frog heaven proudly."

Doci felt those familiar pangs of homesickness. Speaking up he asked aloud, "have you never wanted to return home?"

Logout and Logger exchanged a knowing glance. Logout spoke up. "Doci, we have talked for a long time about returning to Frog Pond. Before you arrived, it was only talk. But Doci, you have inspired all of us with your adventure down here on the Confluence."

Logger moved towards the back of the barn. A large red blanket rested on top of the table. Logger reached for the sheet. "This is what I wanted to show you." In one quick motion he whisked the blanket from the workbench. Dust and wood shavings shot into the air.

Blinking out the sawdust, Doci asked, "what is it?"

"I call it the "GONDOLA," stated Logger proudly.

"It is beautiful," croaked back Doci as he ran his webbed palm along the silky varnished edges. "What is it for?"

Logger smiled and winked at his brother. "My crazy frog-bro gave me the idea. It is sort of a conveyance. There is plenty of room on board for 10-12 frogs."

Doci looked more confused. "What is a conveyance?"

Logger laughed good naturedly. "A conveyance is something that moves a person from one place to another."

Doci looked confused more still. "I don't see wheels or an engine. How does it move?"

Logger smiled, "oh you will see tomorrow. We need to gather up a few more supplies and then we will take the gondola for a spin." Logger brushed some dust off his leather apron. "I got the idea for the gondola from listening to two Crested Larks who once nested on the Laguna Veneta near Venice Italy. They came to be quite familiar with a certain type of river vessel called a gondola. The two-legs have used the gondola to travel around Venice for many centuries. One of the Larks has quite an eye for detail. He watched a gondola being made. It takes a total of 280 interlocking pieces to build the boat. Eight different woods are used – cherry, elm, fir, larch, lime, mahogany, oak, and walnut. I had a real challenge finding lime and mahogany around here for my gondola. Each wood plays a distinct role in the engineering process. Oak is very hard and resistant to the elements. Elm is quite elastic and helps with the curvature of the frame. Fir is resistant to salt water and cherry can be easily bent and molded when we heat the wood. On the front is the metal ferro whose s-shape symbolizes the Great Canal of Venice. The risso on the stern of the boat is said to represent Giudecca Island."

Doci pointed to the middle of the gondola. "What is that structure with the shutters?"

Logger leaned over and pulled on a small cord. The shutters opened up and light streamed into a small cabin. "Have you ever heard of Venetian blinds? The cabin is a felze and is removable. It can protect passengers from the wind and rain but can also be dismantled easily on sunny days. There used to be over 10,000 gondolas in Venice. The larks tell me that nowadays there are barely 400 still in working order. Me being the hopeless romantic that I am,

I wanted to be the first gondolier on the Confluence."

The sun dipped on the horizon. Doci suddenly felt hungry. Reading his guest's stomach grumbles, Logger jumped up. "Where are my manners? Let's get you all moved in to the guesthouse. Food has already been arranged on the back porch. Everyone is going to have to get a good night's sleep and a good meal in their tummy. What an adventure tomorrow brings."

The Statue

Doci woke with the sun's rays filtering through the cobweb curtains. A gentle snorting snore rippled from Logout's corner of the room. With ninja stealth, Doci pattered to the door and out into the dewy morning. The awe of yesterafternoon certainly had not diminished. Doci walked up and down the rows of ligneous animalia. An imposing badger etched in purposeful battle readiness marked the western corner of the army. Sidling up a row of intricately chiseled field mice, Doci hopped gaily eastward. The sculptures seemed to glow gold once bathed in the light of sunrise. So lifelike, the woodland cast emitted an eerie silence. Every size, shape, and woodland form seemed to be accounted for. Fearsome wolves with sharp teeth stood stoically to attention alongside battle-ready stoats and armored rabbits.

Eventually, Doci turned into a small central glade. Unlike all the other carvings, eight large frogs, two on each side of a square, turned inwards towards a central dais. Doci noticed that Logger's army tended to guard with their eyes outward. These eight sentinels looked inward. On closer inspection, Doci marveled at the carved likeness of Logit, LogFarm, Logabin, Logic, Logout, LogDoc, Logjam, and master craftsmen himself, Logger. Each frog engraved in perfect similitude to a living, breathing sibling. The family's armor glistened with every fathomable green precious stone; Verdalite, tsavorite, chrysoprase, malachite, serpentine, prehnite, chrysoberyl, idocrase, kornerupine, variscite, clinochlore, ekanite, chrome sphene, gaspeite, green sapphires, and verdant emeralds. Doci had never before beheld such an array of saturated greens.

Each of the siblings carried an object of notable association. Logit held aloft a gold trophy. LogFarm held up an ornate pitchfork. Logabin extended an arm holding aloft a bricklayer's hod. Logic held a ruler in one hand and an abacus in the other. Logout, armed with a wooden paddle in one arm, extended a ski pole skywards with the other. LogDoc wore a stethoscope around her neck and carried a first aid kit at her side. Instead of armor, the doctor stood clothed in a long green lab coat. Logjam, on the west side of the square carried a humble wooden spoon in one hand and a mixing bowl in the other. Finally, the self-sculpture of Logger loomed several inches larger than his brothers and sisters appropriately armed with a monster hammer and chisel.

Doci followed the statues' gaze. Eight eyes targeted a central carving in the very middle of the wooden army. Two figures stood atop a simply carved tree trunk. Doci felt his breath catch in his throat. The little frog's heart stopped, skipped a beat, and then began to race. "It couldn't be, it can't be, surely not…" Questions raced through Doci's little froggy brain. On the raised platform, sitting on a simple log, sat two familiar personages. Doci closed his eyes. When he opened them, his vision grew fuzzy as tiny iguana-like tears pattered to the ground. The likeness was remarkable and jarring all at the same time. The etching painted a more youthful appearance but there was no mistaking Ma and Pa.

Homecoming

Doci stumbled back to the guesthouse. Could it really be true? Logger stood at the hearth flipping larva-fly pancakes.

"Hey young man, how did you sleep? Did my brother's rumbling snores keep you up all night?"

Doci shook his head. "No, I think all the excitement of these last few weeks caught up on me. I slept like a bullfrog."

Logjam and Logout skipped happily through the door. "Today's the day," chuckled Logout.

"Today's the day for what?" asked Doci.

Logjam wrapped an arm around Doci. Tenderly she squeezed him, "today is the day we go home to Frog Pond."

Doci could hardly contain his excitement. "Frog Pond, but how are we going to get all the way up river. The gondola is amazing but we would need an army of rowers to fight against the current and cross the weir. Then how would we climb the dam?"

Logger flipped a spatula in the air and artfully threw four pancakes down on a plate in front of his bewildered guest. Smiling he said, "who said anything about the gondola going on water? Oh no, this gondola is designed to fly."

****

By the time Logger and his three guests finished breakfast, the sun situated itself very centrally above them. A gentle breeze blew off the river and rusty colored leaves drifted happily to the ground. Autumn came to the Confluence and Mother Nature seemed expectantly happy for the froggy's upcoming adventure.

Logger led the group to the gondola that now sat sturdily on wooden blocks outside the front of the barn. Two frogs were busily stowing supplies on board. Logic and LogDoc turned around and waved enthusiastically.

LogDoc rushed over to hug everyone. "Artur picked us up this morning. He said he would be right back. I think he went to excuse himself from King Egron. He is just as excited about the trip as we are."

Logic spoke kindly to Logjam, "sister, you certainly know how to make friends with the right people. You know a wise frog once said that 'you are the average of the four people you spend the most time with.' LogJam always has a habit of associating with the most kind-hearted souls."

On cue, a powerful beating of wings washed over the group. Doci held on to the sides of the gondola fearful of being blown away. Artur bowed reverently to the group dipping his curved beak to the ground.

Logjam rushed over and threw spindly webbed arms around the eagle's neck. She kissed the bird between the eyes. "Thank you, Artur. You are the noblest in all the sky." Artur cocked his head to the side and winked.

Meanwhile, Logger buzzed industriously around the eagle connecting fine lines to the eagle's saddle and talons.

"What are you doing?" inquired Doci.

"Well," began Logger, "the gondola is going to be carried beneath Artur. I have constructed a beam that Artur can grab with his feet. However, if he grows tired, then I have attached a fail-safe rope across his upper back to stabilize the gondola and to ensure that we don't plummet to the ground. Artur has promised to not fly too high, so we shouldn't be too cold sitting in the airship."

Logout threw one last batch of grub sandwiches in the lunchbox. "Don't want to get hungry up there," he said. "Well let's go get the oldest three. I promised them we would stop by at noon. Logabin and LogFarm slept last night at the Citadel with Logit. Hopefully, they are ready and raring to go."

In moments, the anuran adventurers, found themselves soaring above the Confluence. The gondola swayed timidly in the late morning breeze. The sun sang warmth into the bodies of the travelers. Doci peeked over the edge. Far below him he saw the wooden army disappear. In the east he wistfully surveyed the mountains of the Eyrie. Straining his eyes, he could just make out the powerful wings of Artur's eagle brethren soaring amongst the peaks. Below, the forest ponies ran poetically through the woods. Doci wondered if Emma ran alongside them.

Artur followed the river course. Mischievously, the eagle occasionally dropped low and had the gondola skim the current. River spray drenched the passengers and Artur laughed raucously while the frogs extricated themselves from lunch-bags filled with soggy sandwiches.

Before long, the white tower of the Citadel came into view. Artur circled the spire and then gently brought the gondola down upon a grassy bank adjacent to the river. The unmistakable rotundness of Logabin waved ardently to the travelers. Beside him LogFarm and Logit waited patiently for the ship to land. Logout and Logger leapt over the side to help their older siblings into the vessel. Then with a powerful downbeat of eagle wings, the gondola soared skywards once more.

Doci stood silently transfixed at the bow. He tried to wrap his tiny head around all of the events that had occurred since departing Frog Pond. What an adventure? What a story to tell his family? What a staggering possibility remained ahead? He shook his head and smiled.

"Could it really be?"

Doci tried to follow the river course. High above the ground it seemed impossible to believe that he had traveled so far. Nothing looked familiar. He remembered how difficult and how scared he had been after going over the dam. He reminded himself of a story Ms. Logic had taught him during their lessons together at the school:

Once a rich and powerful king took a large purse of gold coins and hid it in a hole in the center of the road that led to his castle. On top of the hole, he placed a huge boulder. The king hid himself in the bushes to see what would happen. A group of soldiers came by on the way to the castle. They were huge men and very strong. Moving the boulder would have been easy for them, but they believed the task to be beneath them so continued up the road to the castle. Next, a group of merchants passed by. Rather than moving the boulder, they took a very long time circumnavigating the obstacle, complaining loudly about the king and how he was not doing a very good job looking after the roads. Finally, a poor peasant came along. In his arms, he carried a large bushel of vegetables he was hoping to sell at the castle. Seeing the obstacle, he placed down his burden and tried to move the boulder. He pushed, heaved, and strained but couldn't move the boulder. After many hours he finally found a large tree branch that he used as a lever to leverage the boulder up and out of the hole. After rolling the boulder off the road he noticed the purse at the bottom of the hole. Aside from the large reward, a note stated thanks to the person who moved the boulder from the road. In that moment, the king taught a powerful lesson – every hardship and obstacle is a separate opportunity to earn great rewards.

Doci, shut his eyes and reflected on his journey. When he had set out from Frog Pond, he knew nothing of the world beyond the Beaver Dam. Now, he had made eight new friends, become an endurance race champion, learned how to read, met the King of the Eagles, and experienced flight. Not bad for a simple frog from Frog Pond. He had taken the time, energy, and courage to move a boulder.

Doci was still thinking about his big adventure when Logout shouted from the bow,

"I see the Beaver Dam – we are almost home."

Frog Pond

Far from the madding crowd sat Frog Pond. In all of its Waldenesque majesty, the little pond sat serenely captured in time. The gondola on wings of an eagle drifted downwards. With a splish and a splash, the boat touched the crystal blue waters of the pond. A beaver popped his head out of the water.

"Now that is what I call an entrance," he said. "What brings you strangers to this here beaver dam?"

LogFarm popped his head over the starboard side. "I'd recognize that voice anywhere. Hello Mr. Beaver. Do you remember me? I am the oldest son of Mr. and Mrs. Log."

"Well, I'll be a stuffed moose," exclaimed Mr. Beaver. "It has been a decade since the Great Flood. I watched eight sweet children wash over the dam. It broke your parent's hearts it truly did. The Logs tried to start a new family and then they lost another one over the dam a year ago."

"A year ago?" Logabin and Logout popped their heads over the gunwale. Suddenly nine pairs of froggy eyes peered over the edge at Mr. Beaver.

"Well, I'll be a sack of moldy molasses," exclaimed the Beaver. "One, two, three, four, five, six, seven, eight, nine…unbelievable."

Suddenly, Mr. Beaver disappeared under the water.

"What a strange fellow," stated Logabin.

"Where did he go?" asked a perplexed LogDoc.

Logger pointed a finger toward the far bank of the pond. "There he is. It looks like he is dragging a log."

Sure enough, Mr. Beaver paddled towards them at break-neck speed, a large gnarly log in tow. Atop the log, four frogs jumped up and down waving.

Doci, tears in his eyes, dove head first into the water. In a few powerful strokes, he crossed to the log and pulled himself up. You'llsi and We'llsi were on him like ants on honey. "Doci is home" they sang out in unison. I'llsi with a child-like exuberance grabbed his son and together they toppled off the log into the water. Can'tsi, virtually blind from old age and cataracts followed them into the water planting kisses on the prodigal son's head.

The gondola continued to float placidly while the strange reunion played out in the middle of Frog Pond. Mr. Beaver continued to tow the log toward them.

"No, it can't be," stated LogFarm, his voice wavering with emotion. Suddenly, the old farmer flipped overboard and headed out towards the log.

"Has everyone gone mad?" exclaimed Logabin.

The girls were next to have understanding roll over them like a tsunami. Together, Logit, Logic, LogDoc, and Logjam launched acrobatically into Frog Pond. Before Logjam hit the water, one word reverberated around the Beaver dam – "Mom!"

****

The family reunion that followed is a story of legend passed on through the Frog Pond generations. It all needed some sorting out to be sure. Years previously, eight frogs got washed away in the Big Flood. Mr. and Mrs. Log were the only survivors. They had three more children whom they named Doci, We'llsi, and You'llsi. Their eight children had lived for years on the Confluence believing their parents to be dead. Indeed, Logger's wooden army and sculptures had been something of a memorial to his parents.

Doci could not believe his eyes watching mom and dad frolic in the pond with his new-found siblings. Years seemed to wash away from his over-protective parents. We'llsi and

You'llsi, at first extremely shy, now splashed water and wrestled Logout unmercifully through the bulrushes. Doci stretched on the bank in the fading late afternoon sun. Several times he pinched his own arm just to ensure he was not lost in some surreal dream of his own making.

Logjam sidled up beside him and sat staring across the pond.

She tenderly patted Doci's shoulder. "You know, when the floods came, I was so very scared. We all were washed away and separated. Being the youngest, I had never been further than a frog-length from mama. Suddenly, no Frog Pond and I was all alone in the big wide yonder. I got lucky meeting Artur and then he introduced me to King Egron, the Eagle King. He took me in and told me a story that I have never forgotten. Can I tell it now to you?"

Doci nodded and Logjam began her tale:

'Once upon a time, a daughter complained to her father that her life was just too hard. Every time she successfully overcame one challenge,

another seemed to pop up and take its place. She was so tired of fighting and struggling with obstacles. The father, who was a talented chef, took three large pots of water and placed them on the fire. Soon the water started to boil. In the first pot he placed potatoes, in the second pot he threw in some eggs, and in the third he tipped in some ground coffee beans. He let the pots boil while his daughter complained more. After twenty minutes he took the pots from the fire. From the first pot he took potatoes and placed them on a plate. From the second pot he took the eggs and placed them in a bowl. Then from the third pot he ladled coffee into a cup. Turning to his daughter, he asked her, "what do you see?"

She looked at the table and said, "potatoes, eggs, and coffee."

He nodded, and then said, "look closer and touch them." She did so and noticed that the potatoes were now soft. The eggs were now hard and the coffee gave off a beautiful aroma and a taste that made her feel happy.

"I don't understand Father, what does this all mean?" she asked.

He explained that each of the three experienced the same adversity in the boiling water. However, each of the ingredients reacted differently. The potato went in strong and came out soft and weak. The eggs went in fragile and came out hardened. The coffee beans however, were truly unique. When they experienced the obstacle of the boiling water, they changed the water and created something completely new.

Logjam paused for a moment, "Doci which are you? When adversity comes knocking on the door, are you a potato, an egg, or are you the coffee beans? All through life, many events will happen to us and around us, but the true joy of life is what happens within us."

Doci thought for a moment and giggled watching You'llsi dunk an unsuspecting Logabin. "Logjam, I think I have a whole family of coffee beans. I am in awe of my brothers and sisters."

Logjam smiled, "Doci we were all washed over the Beaver Dam and had no choice but to try and make it in the big wide world. Doci, you ***CHOSE*** to leave Frog Pond. We are all in ***AWE*** of ***YOU!***"

During Logjam's story, the other siblings moved up the bank to sit and listen. With Logjam's words followed a wave of nodding heads.

One-by-one, the Frog family came up to Doci and hugged him.

Logit spoke first, "an extraordinary life begins and ends with vigorous movement. To make something from nothing is to ***MOVE***. I am so proud to have a young brother who possesses so much courage and determination. I am glad I could share the Citadel with you."

LogFarm stood up next. "I am not sure you will ever be a farmer, but there are many ways a man can sow seeds. You have farmed hope and love and harvested immeasurable joy by restoring our family.

Logabin followed his brother's lead. "Doci, give a frog a fly and you will feed him for a day. But, teach a frog to catch flies and he will never go hungry again. You have taught me to be brave and not give up. I am so excited to go back to the Confluence and find ways to reunite other families who might have lost loved ones."

Logic stepped forward. "I should have guessed you are a member of the 'Log' family. You are the best student I ever had. Thank you for your curiosity and love of learning. Your spirit of adventure has brought us all home."

Next came Logout. He wrapped Doci in a fierce hug squeezing so hard that the little green frog turned a suffocating shade of blue. "What excitement we had at the waterfall. I should have known we shared the same genetic code for adventure. Remember every day is a separate choice to ***LIVE*** or ***EXIST***. I know my family think I am a little eccentric. But the truth is I just want to feel alive and not waste a single moment. Doci, you have taught me that moments like today should never be taken for granted. Thank you!"

Logout finally released Doci and he let out a massive wheezing sigh of relief. LogDoc, rushed over and rubbed his back with some lavender oil she had retrieved from her medical bag. "If my brother's bungee jumping doesn't put you in the grave, his over-exuberant hugging might. Doci, you have a kind spirit and I just wanted to say thank you for bringing us home."

Logger was the last of the eight siblings to step up. "Well, my young whippersnapper, thank you for helping provide inspiration for my last four carvings. When you come back to visit, I will have them finished." He shook Doci's hand vigorously and stepped back. Doci looked down and realized he held a wooden hand.

"Keep it as a souvenir," laughed Logger.

Mama Log and Papa Log embraced their son. "Doci, we are so proud of you. When you went over the beaver dam, we thought we had lost you too. Instead, you have brought the family back together. Thank you, son."

Epilogue

Frog Pond underwent a startling transformation. Mama and Papa Log, along with Doci's help, opened a summer camp for froglets. Every summer, the family had a big reunion in the new house by the Beaver Dam. Then for four weeks, the siblings entertained campers from miles around. LogFarm and Logjam cooked the food. Logabin built the cabins and organized the campers. Logic taught many different classes and LogDoc was the camp nurse. Logout put his outdoor adventure skills to good use taking the campers on exciting adventures. Logger taught woodworking classes and Logit taught yoga. Doci became the Camp Director and organized all the games and activities.

You'llsi went to college and earned a Marketing diploma. She became so good at designing labels and branding that her siblings re-named her ***"LOGO."*** We'llsi moved down to the Confluence so that Logic could teach him how to read. A natural student, he fell in love with reading and established a new and bigger school library. This literary passion inspired a new name and his family began calling him ***"LOGBOOK."***

In the Fall and Winter months, the whole family moved to the Confluence. Artur flew the gondola up and down the river a few times a year.

Logger resumed his carving project with a passionate industry. On Christmas morning, all the frogs gathered at the Workshop. Logger led his family through the rows of woodland soldiers. Arriving at the center of the square, the frogs noticed four large blankets draped over four new statues. Two statues stood as sentries on either side of the platform. Another statue guarded the front of the dais. The final blanketed creation had been cleverly erected hanging between two trees behind the raised staging occupied by Mama and Papa Log.

Logger, with great pageantry, pulled off the first blanket. Logo dressed in a smart green business suit and a decorative hat looked out on the army. In her right hand she carried a flagstick with the camp emblem blowing in the wind – a mighty eagle with a frog riding on his back.

"That's me," screamed Logo with delight. "I love it." She planted a big kiss on Logger's cheek.

The parallel statue showed off the long and slender Logbook in scholarly graduation robes carrying a scroll in the right hand and a large book in the left.

Logout playfully punched Logbook on the arm. "No fair, your statue is so much more handsome than the real deal."

Everyone laughed. Logger jumped up onto the platform and got up on his tiptoes to remove the third blanket. A hush swallowed the square. Suspended between the trees flew Artur. Only it was not really Artur but a perfect wooden likeness of the Eagle prince. In his talons hung a small reproduction of the Gondola.

Logic spoke first. "Logger it is beautiful. What a gift you have. It is simply magnificent."

"Don't get your nappies in a bunch," Logger laughed happily. "I still have one more carving to unveil. We would not all be here had it not been for Doci."

With the ceremony and deftness of a magician, Logger whipped the final blanket from its post. Underneath – Doci! This statue was so different from the others. Doci wore no armor and no jewels. His simple white shirt and green shorts seemed to be at odds with the elaborate dress of the 999 other carvings.

"Doci, you are one of a kind. I did not want to change one thing about you. You are the one and only original Doci."

Exquisite carving strokes created a perfect likeness of the young frog. A contagious smile filled the round green face. His arms were outstretched in a gesture both welcoming and tender. Between his feet sat the likeness of the Citadel Cup, a potato, a silver nail, a diploma, an acorn helmet, a roll of bandages, some coffee beans, and a wooden hand. The camp logo, with the frog riding an eagle, stretched across his carved white shirt. Doci's hands were open to the sky and his muscular legs and feet anchored him to the earth. For generations afterwards, every visitor to the glade agreed that the statue of Doci represented the most expert craftsmanship of all.

Doci, overcome with emotion, thanked Logger for the honor.

"Speech, speech, speech," everyone cried.

Doci hopped onto the platform and sat cross-legged. "I once met a wise bullfrog named Litho. He gave me a wonderful lesson....

Once upon a time there lived five little frogs. From sunrise to sunset, they sat upon a little log near the river bank. Every day the hot summer sun beat down mercilessly upon their little froggy backs. Sweat poured down tiny arms, perspiration streamed along powerful legs. At precisely 2:00p.m., with the sun at its fiercest, all five frogs decided to jump into the cool water. The question is, at 2:01p.m., how many frogs remained sat upon the log?

*The answer is **FIVE!** You see deciding to jump into the water is not the same as taking action.*

"Every day we get to make choices. We can either choose action or inaction. Action leads to being a coffee bean," Doci smiled at Logjam. "Taking no action means we get stagnant and stop living. My journey down the river introduced me to eight inspirational frogs. These incredible siblings literally transformed my life. I have learned so much. I can now read, build houses, grow potatoes, bandage wounds, cook fly pie, skydive, and run really fast. Every day, I cannot wait to get out of bed to have a new adventure.

Let me leave you with something I taught the campers this summer. We had 100 froglets in the barn. I gave them all a lily pad and asked them to write their names on them. I collected all the lily pads and took them outside and threw them all in the pond. Next, I told the campers to dive into the water and find their lily pad but I gave them only five minutes to do so. Outside – total chaos. Froglets bumped into one another, collided, pushed and shoved. It was not a pretty sight. At the end of five minutes only a few had found their lily pads. I blew my whistle.

I then told every frog to pick up a lily pad and give it to the person whose name appeared on it. In just two minutes, everyone was reunited with their lily pad. This is what the world looks like. Everyone is frantically looking for happiness not being able to find it. This last year, I discovered that my own happiness is connected to the happiness of my friends and family. If I take the time to give lily pads, I will receive lily pads in return. This is the purpose of a happy and meaningful life."

Ten frogs mobbed Doci and he disappeared beneath the hugs of true happiness – FAMILY!

About the Author

Caelin Paul was born in Stevenage, England. He attended Reading Grammar School, the 5th oldest school in Great Britain. From an early age, he was an accomplished athlete and represented his school in athletics, badminton, basketball, chess, cricket, cross-country, rugby, soccer, squash, swimming, tennis, and track. His athletic career took him overseas to Clemson University where he competed in track and field. At Clemson, he was an Atlantic Coast Conference Champion as an 800m runner and an NCAA D1 qualifier.

Paul got his Bachelors and first Master's degree from Clemson University. In 2001, Paul earned his doctorate from the University of Utah and took a teaching position at Southern Virginia University. While in Virginia, he published his first fantasy novel entitled **Child of Night** motivated by his brief association with Orson Scott Card who was teaching at the same college. From 2007 to 2020, Paul taught at Lindenwood University in St. Charles, Missouri. During this time, Paul earned his MA in Professional Counseling and an MBA in Business Leadership. He also served as the University's Head Cross-Country and Track Coach and took three years away to coach the Hong Kong Olympic Track team from 2010 to 2013.

Today, Caelin Paul is a teacher at St. Charles High School. He balances a successful counseling practice with teaching and coaching. **Escape from Frog Pond** introduces the world to a courageous little frog named DOCI who has an extraordinary life adventure teaching the reader about the importance of living over existing.

When not writing, Paul competes in triathlons and goes on big adventures. In 2018 he climbed Kilimanjaro for the second time, in 2019, he competed at the World Ironman Championships in Kona, in 2020, he ran across Great Britain, in 2021, he survived the Antelope Island ultramarathon, and in 2022 he completed the Inca Trail Marathon to Machu Pichu. Like "***Doci***," Caelin Paul likes to frequently escape his own ***"Frog Pond."***

Credits

Some of the stories within the story are adapted from the literary contributions of some great authors who are living "THEIR" lives to the fullest. Here is credit recognition and thanks:

Loren Eiseley – *"The Star Thrower"* published in 1969 in *"The Unexpected Universe"* by Library of America.

Violet Jessup – *"Titanic Survivor: The Memoirs of Violet Jessup, Stewardess"* published in 2007 by the History Press.

Becky Johnen – *"Donkey in the Well"* published in 2017 but adapted from a tale by author unknown.

Daniel Quinn – *"The Story of B"* published in 1996 by Bantam Publishing.

Dulce Rodrigues – *"The Frog's Race"* published in 2020 but adapted from a tale by author unknown.

Credits

Chuck Webster – *"Dream Big: The Words of Truth"* published in Jack Canfield's *"Chicken Soup for the Soul"* – September 2003.

"The King's Road Block" an old tale by an unknown author.

"The Parable of the Potato, Egg, and Coffee Bean" by an unknown author.

"A Picture of Peace" by an unknown author.